"I shall take you back to Italy with me."

Flora's lips parted in a soundless gasp. She stared up at Marco. "You—can't be serious."

"Why not?" He shrugged. "I have to return there, and you need to escape. It solves several problems."

And creates a hundred others. She thought it, but did not say it. She said slowly, "Marco—why do you want me with you?"

He put his lips to the agitated pulse in her throat. "You have a short memory, *mia cara.* Do you really not know?"

Sara Craven

THE FORCED MARRIAGE

ITALIAN HUSBANDS

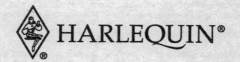

HARLEQUIN®

TORONTO • NEW YORK • LONDON
AMSTERDAM • PARIS • SYDNEY • HAMBURG
STOCKHOLM • ATHENS • TOKYO • MILAN • MADRID
PRAGUE • WARSAW • BUDAPEST • AUCKLAND

ISBN 0-373-12320-5

THE FORCED MARRIAGE

First North American Publication 2003.

Copyright © 2002 by Sara Craven.

This edition published by arrangement with Harlequin Books S.A.

Visit us at www.eHarlequin.com

Printed in U.S.A.

CHAPTER ONE

'TELL me something,' said Hester. 'Are you absolutely certain you want to get married?'

Flora Graham, whose thoughts had drifted to the on-going knotty problem of informing those concerned that she didn't want her spoiled and brattish nephew as a pageboy, hurriedly snapped back to the immediate present, the crowded and cheerful restaurant, and her best friend and bridesmaid eyeing her with concern across the table.

'Of course I do.' She frowned slightly. 'Chris and I are perfect for each other; you know that. I couldn't be happier.'

'You don't look particularly happy,' Hester said judicially, refilling their coffee cups.

Flora rolled her eyes in mock despair. 'You wait until it's your turn, and you find yourself in the middle of a three-ring circus with no time off for good behaviour. My mother must have been having one of her deaf days when I said I wanted a small quiet wedding.'

'Then why don't you have one?' Hester met her astonished look steadily. 'Why don't you ask Chris to get a special licence, and slope off somewhere and do the business? I'll happily be one witness, and maybe Chris's best man would be the other.'

Flora went on staring at her. 'Because we can't. We're committed to all these arrangements—all that expense. We'd be letting so many people down. It's too late.'

'Honey, it's never too late.' Hester's voice was persuasive. 'And I'm sure most people would understand.'

Flora gave a wry shake of the head. 'Not my mother,' she said. *And, my God, certainly not Chris's.* 'Anyway, don't you want to do your bridesmaid thing? I've arranged for you to catch my bouquet afterwards.'

'Having observed you closely since the engagement party, I think I'll pass,' Hester said drily. 'I'm not ready for a nervous breakdown.' She paused. 'Talking of engagements, I see you're not wearing your ring. Would that be a Freudian slip?'

'No, I damaged a claw in the setting last week, and it's being repaired.' Flora's frown deepened. 'What is this, Hes? You're beginning to sound as if you don't like Chris.'

'That's not true,' her friend said slowly. 'But, even if you hate me for ever, I have to tell you I think you could do better.'

Flora gasped. 'You don't mean that. I *love* Chris, in case you hadn't noticed.'

Hester was silent for a moment. 'Flo, in all the years we've known each other I've seen you with various men, but never in a serious relationship with any of them. Although that's fine,' she added hastily. 'You've never slept around, and I admire you for sticking to your principles. *But* I always thought that when you fell, you'd fall hard. Passion to die for—heaven, hell and heartbreak—the works. And I don't see much sign of that with you and Chris.'

'I'm glad to hear it,' Flora said calmly. 'It sounds very uncomfortable.'

'But it should be uncomfortable,' Hester returned implacably. 'Love isn't some cosy old coat that you slip on because it's less trouble than shopping for a new one.'

'But that isn't how I feel at all,' Flora protested. 'I—I'm crazy about him.'

'Really?' Hester was inexorable. 'In that case, why aren't you living together?'

'The flat needs work—decoration. We want it to be perfect. After all, it's going to be my showcase, and it's taking longer than we thought.' Flora realised with exasperation how feeble that sounded.

'That,' said Hester, 'hardly suggests that you can't keep your hands off each other. And I suppose the cost of refurbishment prevents you sneaking off together for a romantic weekend in the country?'

'When we're married,' Flora said defiantly, 'every weekend will be romantic.'

'Be honest, now.' Hester leaned forward. 'If Chris came to you tomorrow and said he wanted to call it off, would it be the end of your world?'

'Yes.' Flora lifted her chin. 'Yes, it would.' She paused. 'Perhaps Chris and I aren't the most demonstrative couple in the world, but who says you have to wear your heart on your sleeve?'

'Sometimes,' Hester said gently, 'you simply can't help yourself.' She drank the rest of her coffee and reached for her bag, and the bill. 'However, if that's how you really feel, and you're sure about it, there's no more to be said.' She pushed back her chair. 'On the other hand, if you ever have doubts about what you're doing, I'll be around to pick up the pieces. Sal the demon flatmate is off to Brussels for three months, so I've a spare room again.'

'It's a sweet offer,' Flora said gently. 'And I don't hate you for making it, even though it's not necessary.'

She gave Hester an affectionate grin. 'I thought it was supposed to be the bride who got the pre-wedding jitters, not the bridesmaid.'

'I'd be happier if you were jittery,' Hester retorted. 'You act as though you're resigned to your fate. And there's no need to be. You're gorgeous and the world is full of attractive men waiting to be attracted.' She dropped a swift kiss on Flora's hair as she went past. 'And, if you don't believe me, check out the guy over there at the corner table,' she added in sepulchral tones. 'He's had his eyes on you all through lunch.' And, with a conspiratorial wink, she was gone.

Flora ought to have left too. Instead she found she was reaching for the cafetière and refilling her cup again. Maybe she should include sugar this time, she thought, biting her lip. Wasn't that one of the treatments for shock?

Because she couldn't pretend that Hester's blunt remarks had just slid off her consciousness like water off a duck's back.

Stunned, she thought wryly, is the appropriate word.

And all from an innocuous girlie lunch to make a final decision between old rose and delphinium-blue for Hester's dress.

Unbelievable.

And it wasn't the drink talking either. *In vino veritas* hardly applied to a glass of Chardonnay apiece and a litre of mineral water.

No, it was clear this had been brewing for some time, and, with a month to go before the wedding, Hester had decided it was time to speak her mind.

But I really wish she hadn't, Flora thought, biting her lip. I was perfectly content when I sat down at this table. And I've enough on my mind without doing a detailed analysis of my feelings for Chris, and seeing how they measure on some emotional Richter scale I never knew existed.

I love Chris, and I know we're going to have a good marriage—one that will last, too. And surely that matters far more than—sexual fireworks.

She felt her mind edging gently away from that particular subject, and paused quite deliberately. Because that would also be all right once they were married, she reassured herself, and that previous fiasco would be entirely forgotten.

She glanced at her watch and rose. Time was pressing, and she would have to take a cab to her next appointment.

On her way out of the restaurant she remembered Hester's parting remarks and risked a swift sideways glance at the table in question. Only to find herself looking straight into the eyes of its occupant.

He was very dark, she registered as she looked away, her face warming with embarrassment, with curling hair worn longer than she approved of. He was also startlingly attractive, in an olive-skinned Mediterranean way. The image of an elegant high-bridged nose, sculptured cheekbones, a firm chin with a cleft in it, and a mobile mouth that quirked sensuously under her regard accompanied her out of the restaurant and into the sunlit street beyond.

My God, she realised, half-amused, half-concerned. I could practically draw him from memory.

And, damn you, Hes. That was something else I didn't need.

She stepped to the edge of the kerb and looked down the street for an approaching taxi. But there wasn't one in sight, so she started to walk in the required direction, pausing every now and then to look back.

She didn't even see her assailant coming. The first hint of danger was a hand in her back, pushing her violently, and a wrench at the strap of her bag that nearly dragged it from her grasp.

Flora felt herself go sprawling, the bag pinned underneath her, as she filled her lungs and screamed for help. On the ground, she covered her head with her hands, terrified that she was going to be punched or kicked.

Then she heard men's voices shouting, a squeal of brakes, and the sound of running feet.

Flora stayed still, exactly where she was, the breath sobbing in her throat.

She could hear someone speaking to her in husky, faintly accented English.

'Are you hurt, *signorina*? Shall I call an ambulance for you? Can you speak?'

'She may not talk, mate, but she can yell. Nearly took me eardrums out,' said a deeper, gruffer voice. 'Let's see if we can get her to her feet.'

'It's all right.' Flora raised her head dazedly and looked around her. 'I can manage.'

'I don't think so.' The first voice again. 'I believe you must accept a little help, *signorina*.'

Flora turned unwillingly in the speaker's direction, to have all her worst fears confirmed.

Seen at close range—and he was kneeling beside her so he could hardly have been any closer—the man from the restaurant was even more devastating. His mouth was set grimly now, but she could imagine how it would soften. And his eyes, she had leisure to note, were green, with tiny gold flecks. A whisper of some expensive male cologne reached her, and, suddenly keen to get out of range of its evocative scent, Flora hauled herself up on to her knees.

'Ouch.' Major mistake, she thought, wincing. She'd ripped her tights and grazed her legs when she fell. Her elbows and palms were sore too.

'Come on, ducks.' It was Voice Two. A burly arm went round her, lifting her bodily to her feet. 'Why don't I pop you in the cab and take you to the nearest casualty department, eh?'

'Cab?' Flora repeated. 'I—I wanted a cab.'

'Well, I could see that, and I was just pulling over when that bastard jumped you. Then this other gentleman came flying up, and the mugger legged it.'

'Oh.' Flora made herself look at the 'other gentleman', who stood, smiling faintly, those astonishing eyes trailing over her in a cool and disturbingly thorough assessment. 'Well—thank you.'

He inclined his head gravely. 'Your bag is safe? And he took nothing else?'

'He didn't really get the chance.' She gave him a brief, formal smile, then turned to the cabbie. 'I need to go to Belvedere Row. I'm supposed to be meeting someone there and I'm going to be late.'

'I hardly think you can keep your appointment like that,' her rescuer intervened firmly. 'At the least you require a clothes brush, and your cuts should also be attended to.'

Before she could protest Flora found herself manoeuvred into the back of the cab, with the stranger taking the seat beside her.

'The Mayfair Tower Hotel, please,' he directed the driver.

'I can't go there.' Flora shot bolt upright. 'My appointment's in the other direction.'

'And when you are clean and tidy, another cab will take you there.' An autocratic note could be detected in the level tone. 'It is a business meeting? Then it is simple. You call on your cellphone and explain why you are delayed.'

'So what's it to be, love?' the driver demanded through the partition. 'The Mayfair Tower?'

Flora hesitated. 'Yes—I suppose.'

'A wise decision,' her companion applauded smoothly.

She sent him a steely glance. 'Do you enjoy arranging other people's lives?'

His answering smile warmed into a grin. 'Only those that I have saved,' he drawled.

Deep within her an odd tingle stirred uneasily. She tried to withdraw unobtrusively, further into her corner of the taxi.

'Isn't that rather an exaggeration?'

He shrugged powerful shoulders that the elegant lines of his charcoal suit accentuated rather than diminished. The top button of his pale grey silk shirt was undone, Flora noticed, and the knot of his ruby tie loosened. For the rest of him, he was about six feet tall, lean and muscular, with legs that seemed to go on for ever.

He wasn't merely attractive, she acknowledged unwillingly. He was seriously glamorous.

'Then let's say I spared you the inconvenience of losing your credit cards and money. To many people, that would be life and death.'

She smiled constrainedly. 'And my engagement ring is at the jeweller's, so really I've got off lightly.'

That was clumsily done, she apostrophised herself silently, and saw by his sardonic smile that he thought so too.

She hurried into speech again. 'Why the Mayfair Tower?'

'I happen to be staying there.'

There was a silence, then she said, 'Then you must let me drop you off before I take this cab back to my flat, to clean up and change.'

'You are afraid I shall make unwelcome advances to you?' His brows lifted. 'Allow me to reassure you. I never seduce maidens in distress—unless, of course, they insist.'

Her mouth tightened. 'I dare say you think this is very amusing…'

'On the contrary, *signorina*, I take the whole situation with the utmost seriousness.' For a moment, there was an odd note in his voice.

Then he added with cool courtesy, 'You are trying to shrug off what has happened, but you have had a severe shock and that will bring its own reaction. I do not think you should be alone.'

'You're very kind,' Flora said tautly. 'But I really can't go with you. You must see that.'

'I seem to be singularly blind this afternoon.' He took a slim wallet from an inside pocket of his jacket and extracted a card. 'Perhaps a formal introduction may convince you of my respectability.'

Flora accepted the card and studied it dubiously. 'Marco Valante,' she read. And beneath it 'Altimazza Inc'. She glanced up. 'The pharmaceutical company?'

'You have heard of us?' His brows lifted.

'Of course.' She swallowed. 'You're incredibly successful. Whenever your shares are offered my fiancé recommends them to his clients.'

'He is a broker, perhaps?' he inquired politely.

'An independent financial adviser.'

'Ah, and do you work in the same area?'

'Oh, no,' Flora said hastily. 'I'm a consultant in property sales.'

His brows rose. 'You sell houses?'

'Not directly. The agencies hire me to show people how to present their properties to the best advantage when potential buyers are going round. I get them to refurbish tired décor—or tone down strident colour schemes.'

'I imagine that would not always be easy.'

She smiled reluctantly. 'No. We have a saying that an Englishman's home is his castle, and sometimes sellers are inclined to pull up the drawbridge. I have to convince them that their property is no longer a loved home but a commodity which they want to sell at a profit. Sometimes it takes a lot of persuasion.'

He looked at her reflectively. 'I think,' he said softly, 'that you could persuade a monk to abandon his vows, *mia cara*.'

Flora stiffened. 'Please—don't say things like that.'

He pantomimed astonishment. 'Because you are to be married you can no longer receive compliments from other men? How quaint.'

'That,' she said, 'is not what I meant.'

Totally relaxed in his own corner, he grinned at her. 'And you must not be teased either? *Si, capisce.* From now on I will behave like a saint.'

He didn't look like a saint, Flora thought. More like a rebel angel...

She glanced back at the card he had given her. 'You don't look like a chemist,' she said, and almost added *either*.

'I'm not.' He pulled a face. 'I work in the accounting

section, mainly raising funding for our research projects.'

'Oh,' she said. 'Well—that would explain it.'

Actually, it explained nothing, because he wasn't her idea of an accountant either, by a mile and a half.

'Does everything have to be readily comprehensible?' he enquired softly. 'Do you never wish to embark on a long, slow voyage of discovery?'

Flora had the feeling that he was needling her again, but she refused to react. 'I'm more used to first impressions—instant reactions. It's part of my job.'

'So,' he said. 'You know who I am. Will you grant me the same privilege?'

'Oh,' she said. 'Yes—of course…'

She delved into her misused bag and produced one of her own business cards. He read it, then looked back at her, those amazing eyes glinting under their heavy lids. 'Flora,' he said softly. 'The goddess of the springtime.'

She flushed and looked away. 'Actually, I was named after my grandmother—far more prosaic.'

'So, tell me—Flora—will you continue to work after you are married?'

'Naturally.'

'You are sure that your man will not guard you even more closely when you are his wife?'

'That's nonsense,' Flora said indignantly. 'Chris doesn't *guard* me.'

'Good,' Marco Valante said briskly. 'Because we have arrived at the hotel, and there is nothing, therefore, to prevent you going in with me.'

Flora had every intention of offering him a last haughty word of thanks, then hobbling out of his life for ever. But suddenly the commissionaire was there, help-

ing her out of the taxi and holding open the big swing
doors so she could go in.

And then she was in the foyer, all marble and plate
glass, and Marco Valante had joined her and was giving
soft-voiced orders that people were hurrying to obey—
a lot of them concerning herself.

And suddenly the reality of making the kind of scene
which would extract her from this situation seemed totally beyond her capabilities.

In fact, she was forced to acknowledge, all she really
wanted to do was find somewhere quiet and burst into
tears.

She didn't even utter a protest when she was escorted
to the lift and taken up to the first floor. She walked
beside Marco Valante to the end of the corridor, and
waited while he slotted in his key card and opened the
door.

Mutely, she preceded him into the room.

Although this was no mere room, she saw at once. It
was a large and luxuriously furnished suite, and they
were standing in the sitting room. The curtains were half
drawn, to exclude the afternoon sun, and he went over
and flung them wide.

'Sit down.' He indicated one of the deeply cushioned
sofas and she sank down on it with unaccustomed obe-
dience, principally because her throbbing legs were
threatening to give way beneath her.

'I have told them to send the nurse here to dress your
cuts,' he said. 'I have also ordered some tea for you, and
if you go into the bathroom you will find a robe you can
wear while your suit is being valeted.'

She said shakily, 'You're pretty autocratic for an accountant.'

He shrugged. 'I wish to make some kind of amends for what happened earlier.'

'I don't see why,' Flora objected. 'It wasn't your fault.'

'But I could, perhaps, have prevented it if I had been quicker. If I had obeyed my instinct and left the restaurant when you did.'

'Why should you do that?' Reaction was beginning to set in. She felt deathly cold suddenly, and wrapped her arms round her body, gritting her teeth to stop them from chattering.

'I thought,' he said softly, 'that I was not permitted to pay you compliments. But, if you must know, I wanted very much to make the acquaintance of a beautiful girl with hair that Titian might have painted.'

So Hes had been right, Flora realised with a little jolt of shock. He had indeed been watching her during lunch.

'Presumably,' she said, with an effort, 'you have a thing about red-haired women.'

'Not until today, when I saw you in the sunlight, Flora *mia*.'

For a moment her heart skipped a treacherous beat, before reason cut in and she wondered with intentional cynicism how many other women that particular line had worked with.

She closed her eyes, deliberately shutting him out. Using it as a form of rejection.

While at the same time she thought, 'I should not—I *really* should not be here.'

And only realised she had spoken aloud when he said quietly, 'Yet you are perfectly safe. For at any moment people will start arriving, and I shall probably never be alone with you again.'

And never, mourned a small voice in her head, is such

a very long time. And such a very lonely word. But that was a thought she kept strictly to herself.

She said, 'Perhaps you'd show me where the bathroom is.'

She had, inevitably, to cross his bedroom to reach it, and she followed him, her eyes fixed rigidly on his back, trying not to notice the kingsize bed with its sculptured ivory coverlet.

The bathroom was all creamy tiles edged with gold, and she stood at a basin shaped like a shell and took her first good look at herself, her lips shaping into a silent whistle of dismay.

Shock had drained her normally pale skin and she looked like a ghost, her clear grey eyes wide and startled. There was a smudge on her cheek, and her shirt was dirty and ripped, exposing several inches of lacy bra. Which Marco Valante was bound to have noticed, she thought, biting her lip.

Well, perhaps the valeting service could lend her a safety pin, she told herself as she removed her suit and carefully peeled off her torn tights.

She washed her face and hands, then did her best to make herself look less waif-like with the powder and lipstick in her bag, before turning her attention to her unruly cloud of dark red hair.

Usually, for work, she stifled its natural wave, drawing it severely back from her face and confining it at the nape of her neck with a barrette or a bow of dark ribbon. Although a few tendrils invariably managed to escape and curl round her face.

But today the ribbon had gone, allowing the whole gleaming mass to tumble untrammelled round her shoulders, and no amount of struggling with a comb could restore it to its normal control.

But then nothing was normal today, she thought with a sigh, as she put on the oversized towelling robe and secured its sash round her slim waist. It covered her completely, but she still felt absurdly self-conscious as she made her way back to the sitting room.

Only it was not Marco Valante awaiting her but the nurse, a brisk blonde in a neat navy uniform, clearly more accustomed to reassuring elderly tourists about their digestive problems. But she cleaned Flora up with kindly efficiency, putting antiseptic cream and small waterproof dressings over the worst of her grazes.

'You don't expect that kind of thing,' she remarked, giving her handiwork a satisfied nod. 'Not in a busy street in broad daylight. And why you, anyway? You're hardly wearing a Rolex or dripping with gold.'

Flora agreed rather wanly. The same question had been nagging at her too. After all, she wasn't the world's most obvious target. Just one of those random chances, she supposed. Being in the wrong place at the wrong time.

But, if it came to that, she was still in the wrong place, with no escape in sight.

Marco Valante had tactfully withdrawn while she was receiving attention, but now Room Service had arrived, bringing the tea, and he would undoubtedly be rejoining her at any moment.

And she would have to start thanking him all over again, she thought with vexation, because along with the tea had been delivered a carrier bag, bearing the name of a famous store, containing not only a fresh pair of tights but a new white silk shirt as well. Even more disturbingly, both of them were in her correct size, confirming her suspicion that this was a man who knew far too much about women.

Accordingly, her smile was formal and her greeting subdued when he came back into the sitting room.

'Are you feeling better?' The green eyes swept over her, as if the thick layer of towelling covering her had somehow ceased to exist. As if every inch of her body was intimately familiar to him, she thought as her heart began to thud in mingled excitement and panic.

'Heavens, yes. As good as new.' From some unfathomed corner of her being she summoned up a voice so spuriously hearty that she cringed with embarrassment at herself.

'And the hotel assures me your clothes will soon be equally pristine.' He seated himself opposite to her. 'They are being dealt with as a matter of priority.' He paused. 'But it seemed to me that your blouse was beyond help.'

Flora said a stilted, 'Yes', aware that her face had warmed. She reached for her bag. 'You must let me repay you.'

'With the greatest pleasure,' he said. He shrugged off his jacket and tossed it across the arm of the sofa, unbuttoned his waistcoat with deft fingers, then leaned back against the cushions, the lean body totally at ease. 'Have dinner with me tonight.'

Flora gasped. 'I couldn't possibly.'

'*Perche no?* Why not?'

'I told you.' Her colour deepened, seemed to envelop her entire body. 'I'm engaged to be married.'

He shrugged. 'You already told me. What of it?'

'Doesn't it matter to you?'

'Why should it? I might be *fidanzato* also.'

'Well—are you?'

'No.' Had she imagined an oddly harsh note in his voice? 'I am a single man, *mia bella*. But it would make no difference.' He paused, the green eyes sardonic. 'After all, I am not suggesting we should have our dinner served in bed.'

He allowed that to sink in, then added silkily, 'Do you feel sufficiently safe to pour the tea?'

'Of course.' Flora dragged some remaining shreds of composure around her. 'Milk and sugar?'

'Lemon only, I thank you.'

By some miracle she managed to manoeuvre the heavy teapot so that its contents went only into the delicate porcelain cups and not all over the tray, the table, and the carpet, but it was a close-run thing, and her antennae told her that Marco Valante was perfectly well aware of her struggles and privately amused by them.

She handed him his cup, controlling an impulse to pour the tea straight in his lap.

He accepted it with a brief word of thanks. 'Did you telephone your clients?'

'Yes.' An impersonal topic, she thought thankfully. 'They were very forgiving and rescheduled.'

'You do not think your *fidanzato* would be equally understanding, and spare you to me—for one evening?'

She gasped. 'I know he wouldn't.'

'Strange,' Marco Valante said musingly. 'Because he cannot be so very possessive.'

'Why do you say that?'

He smiled at her. 'Because he has never—possessed you, *mia bella*.'

Flora gasped in outrage. 'How dare you say such a thing?'

'When possible, I prefer to speak the truth. And I say that you are still—untouched.'

'You—you can't possibly know that,' she said hoarsely. 'And it's none of your business anyway.'

'Destiny has caused our paths to cross, Flora *mia*,' he said softly. 'I think I am entitled to be a little—intrigued when I look into your eyes and see there no woman's knowledge—no memory of desire.'

She replaced her cup on the tray with such force that it rattled. She said tautly, 'Actually, you have no rights at all. And I'd like to leave now, please.'

'Like that?' His brows lifted. 'You will be a sensation, *cara*.'

She said, her voice shaking, 'I'd rather walk down the street naked than have to endure any more of your— humiliating—and inaccurate speculation about my personal life.'

Marco Valante smiled. 'I am tempted to make you prove it, but I am feeling merciful today. I will arrange for you to have the use of another room while you wait for your clothes.'

He picked up the phone, dialled a number and spoke briefly and succinctly.

'A maid will come and take you to your new sanctuary,' he told her pleasantly when he had finished. He pulled a leather-covered notepad towards him and scribbled a few lines on the top sheet, which he tore off and handed to her. 'If you change your mind about dinner you may join me at this restaurant any time after eight o'clock.'

She crushed the paper into a ball and dropped it to the floor. She said, coldly and clearly, 'Hell will freeze over first, *signore*.'

His own voice was soft, almost reflective. 'So the flame does not burn in your hair alone. *Bravo*.'

She snatched up the shirt and tights, glaring at him, unbearably galled that she needed to use them, and crammed them into her bag.

'I'll send you a cheque for these,' she told him curtly.

Marco Valante laughed. 'I'm sure you will, *cara*. But in case you forget, I'll take a down payment now.'

Suddenly he was beside her, and his arm was round her, pulling her towards him. And for one brief, burning moment, she felt his mouth on hers, tasting her with a stark hunger she had never known existed.

It was over almost as soon as it had begun. Before she'd really grasped what was happening to her she was free, stepping backwards, stumbling a little on the edge of that trailing robe, staring at him in a kind of horror as her hand went up to touch her lips.

And he looked back at her, his own mouth twisting wryly. He said quietly, 'As hot as sin and as sweet as honey. I cannot wait for the next instalment, Flora *mia*.'

The note in his voice seemed to shiver on her skin. The silence between them tautened—became electric. She wanted to look away, and found that she could not.

It was the knock on the door that saved her. She went to answer it, holding up the encumbering folds of towelling, trying not to run.

His voice followed her. '*Ti vedrò, mia bella*. I'll be seeing you.'

She said fiercely, 'No—no, you won't.'

And went through the door, slamming it behind her, because she knew, to her shame, that she did not dare look back at him. Not then. And certainly not ever again.

CHAPTER TWO

'I GOT you a herb tea,' Melanie said anxiously. 'As you still can't face cappuccino. They say shock can do that to you.'

Some shocks certainly could, Flora thought grimly as she took the container from her assistant with a word of thanks and a smile. Nor was it just cappuccino. She was also off espresso, latte and anything else tall and Italian.

Three jumpy days had passed since the aborted mugging and its even more disturbing aftermath. Out of the frying pan, she thought wryly, and into the heart of the fire. She was still screening her calls, and warily scanning the streets outside her flat and office each time she emerged.

'I'll be seeing you,' he'd said. The kind of casual remark anyone might make, and probably meaningless. An unfortunate choice of words, that was all. And yet— and yet...

He had made it sound like a promise.

Time and time again she told herself she was a fool for letting it matter so much. Her grazes, bumps and bruises were healing nicely, and she should let her emotions settle too. Put the whole thing in some mental recycling bin.

It had been obvious from that first moment that Marco Valante was trouble, and it was her bad luck that he should have been the first on the scene when she needed help. Because he was the kind of man to whom flirting was clearly irresistible, and who would allow no opportunity to be wasted.

But—it was only a kiss, when all was said and done, she thought, taking a rueful sip of herb tea. And wasn't this a total overreaction on her part to something he would undoubtedly have forgotten by now?

He would have moved on—might even be back in Italy and good riddance—and she should do the same. So why on earth was it proving so difficult? Why was he invading her thoughts by day and her sleep by night? It made no sense.

And, more importantly, why hadn't she told Chris all about it? she asked herself, staring unseeingly at her computer screen.

Partly, she supposed, because his attitude had annoyed her. He'd been sympathetic at first, but soon become bracing, telling her she was lucky not to have lost her bag or been badly injured. She knew she'd got off lightly, but somehow that wasn't what she'd needed to hear. Some prolonged concern and cosseting would have been far more acceptable. And it would have been for her to tell him, lovingly, that he was going OTT, and not the other way round.

He was busy, of course, and she understood that. He was trying to build up his consultancy and provide a sound financial basis for their future; she couldn't realistically expect his attention to be focussed on her all the time.

But she had anticipated that he'd stay with her that evening at least.

Instead, 'Sorry, my sweet.' Chris had shaken his head. 'I've arranged to meet a new client. Could be big. Besides,' he'd added, patting her shoulder, 'you'll be much better off relaxing—taking things easy. You don't need me for that.'

No, Flora had thought, with a touch of desolation. But I could do with the reassurance of your arms around me. I'd like you to look at me as *he* did. To let me know that you want me, that you're living for our wedding, and the moment when we'll really belong to each other.

And that it won't be like that other time...

She bit her lip, remembering, then turned her attention firmly back to the report she was writing for a woman trying to sell an overcrowded, overpriced flat in Notting Hill. Although she suspected she was wasting her time and Mrs Barstow would not remove even one of the small occasional tables which made her drawing room an obstacle course, or banish her smelly, bad-tempered Pekinese dog on viewing days.

She would probably also quibble at the fee she was being charged, Flora decided as she printed up the report and signed it.

She turned to the enquiries that had come in recently, remembering that Melanie had marked one of them urgent. 'Lady living in Chelsea,' she said now. 'A Mrs Fairlie. Husband does something in the EU and they're having to move to Brussels like yesterday, so she needs to spruce the place up for a quick sale. Says we were recommended.'

'That's what I like to hear,' Flora commented as she dialled Mrs Fairlie's number.

She liked the sound of Mrs Fairlie too, who possessed a rich, deep voice with a smile in it, but who sounded clearly harassed when Flora mentioned she had no vacant appointments until the following week.

'Oh, please couldn't you fit me in earlier?' she appealed. 'I'd like you to see the house before matters go any further, and time is pressing.'

Flora studied her diary doubtfully. 'I could maybe call in on my way home this evening,' she suggested. 'If that's not too late for you.'

'Oh, no,' Mrs Fairlie said eagerly. 'That sounds ideal.'

Flora replaced the receiver and sat for a moment, lost in thought. Then she reached for the phone again and, acting on an impulse she barely understood, dialled the Mayfair Tower Hotel.

'I'm trying to trace a Signor Marco Valante,' she invented. 'I believe he is staying at your hotel.'

'I am sorry, madam, but Signor Valante checked out yesterday.' Was there a note of regret in the receptionist's professional tone?

'Oh, okay, thanks,' Flora said quickly.

She cut the connection, aware that her heart was thudding erratically—with what had to be relief. He was safely back in Italy and she had nothing more to worry about from that direction, thank goodness.

I've got to stop being so negative, she thought. Take some direct action about the future. I'll have a blitz on the flat this weekend, and persuade Chris to help me. Even if he hates decorating he can lend a hand in preparing the walls. And we'll finalise arrangements for the wedding too. A few positive steps and I'll be back in the groove. No time to fill my head with rubbish.

She took a cab to the quiet square where Mrs Fairlie lived that evening, appraising the house with a faint frown as she paid off the driver. It was elegant, double fronted, and immaculately maintained. And clearly worth a small fortune.

Flora would have bet good money that even if the entire interior was painted in alternating red and green stripes the queue of interested buyers would still stretch round the block.

And if Mrs Fairlie simply wanted reassurance that her property was worth the amazing amount the agents were advising, then reassurance she should have, Flora decided with a mental shrug as she rang the bell.

The door was answered promptly by a pretty maid in a smart chocolate-coloured uniform, who smiled and nodded when Flora introduced herself, and led her up a wide curving staircase to the drawing room on the first floor.

As she followed, Flora was aware of the elegant ceramic floor in the hall, the uncluttered space and light enhanced by clean pastel colours on the walls. As she'd suspected, she thought wryly, Mrs Fairlie was the last person to need style advice.

The maid opened double doors, and after announcing, 'Miss Graham,' stood back to allow Flora to precede her into the room.

She was greeted by the dazzle of evening sunlight from the tall windows, and halted, blinking, conscious that amid the glare someone was moving towards her.

But not the female figure she'd been expecting, she realised with a jolt, the confident, professional smile dying on her lips.

In spite of the warmth of the room she felt as cold as ice. She had to fight an impulse to wrap her arms across her body in a betrayingly defensive gesture.

'*Buonasera*, Flora *mia*.' As Marco Valante reached her he captured her nerveless hand and raised it swiftly and formally to his lips. 'It is good to see you again.'

'I wish I could say the same.' Her voice sounded husky and a little breathless. 'What is this? I came here to meet a Mrs Fairlie.'

'Unfortunately she has been detained. But she has delegated me to show you the house in her absence.'

'And you expect me to believe that?'

His brows lifted sardonically. 'What else, *cara*? Do you imagine I have her bound and gagged in the cellar?'

Something very similar had occurred to her, and she lifted her chin, glaring at him. 'I find it odd that you have the run of her house, certainly.'

'I am staying here for a few days,' he said calmly. 'Your Mrs Fairlie is in fact my cousin Vittoria.'

'I see.' Her heart seemed to be trying to beat its way out of her ribcage. 'And you persuaded her to trick me into coming here. Does your family claim descent from Machiavelli?'

'I think he was childless,' Marco Valante said thoughtfully. 'And Vittoria did not need much persuasion—not when I explained how very much I wished to meet with you again.' He smiled. 'She tends to indulge me.'

'More fool her,' Flora said curtly. 'I'd like to leave, please. Now.'

'Before you have carried out your survey of the house?' He tutted reprovingly. 'Not very professional, *cara*.'

She sent him a freezing look. 'But then I hardly think I've been inveigled into coming here in my business capacity.'

'You are wrong. Vittoria wishes your advice on the master bedroom. She is bored with the colour, and the main bedroom in her house in Brussels has been decorated in a similar shade.'

Flora frowned. 'She is genuinely selling this house, then?'

'It has already been sold privately,' he said gently. 'Shall we go upstairs?'

'*No!*' The word seemed to explode from her with such force that her throat ached.

She saw him fling his head back as if she had struck him in the face. Met the astonishment and scorn in the green eyes as they held hers. Felt the ensuing silence deepen and threaten, as if some time bomb were ticking away. And realised with swift shame that she had totally overstepped the mark.

Somehow, she faltered into speech. 'I'm sorry—I didn't mean...'

He said grimly, 'I am not a fool. I know exactly what you meant.' The long fingers captured her chin and held it, not gently. 'Two things, *mia cara*.' He spoke softly. 'This is my cousin's house, and I would not show such disrespect for her roof. More importantly, I have never yet taken a woman against her will—and you will not be the first. *Capisce?*'

Her face burned as, jerkily, she nodded.

'Then be good enough to carry out the commission you've been employed for.' He released her almost contemptuously and moved towards the door. 'Shall I call Malinda to act as our chaperon?'

'No,' she said huskily. 'That—won't be necessary.' Her legs were shaking as she ascended another flight of stairs to the second floor, and followed him into Vittoria Fairlie's bedroom.

It was a large room, overlooking the garden, with French windows leading on to a balcony with a wrought-iron balustrade and ceramic containers planted brightly with flowers.

The interior walls were the palest blush pink, with stinging white paintwork as a contrast, and the tailored bedcover was a much deeper rose. Apart from a chaise longue near the window, upholstered in the same fabric as the bedcover, and an elegant walnut dressing table, there was little other furniture—all clothes and clutter having been banished, presumably, to the adjoining dressing room.

'Well?' Marco Valante had stationed himself at the window, leaning against its frame. So how was it that everywhere she looked he seemed to be in her sightline? she wondered despairingly.

The image of him seemed scored into her consciousness—the casual untidiness of his raven hair, the faint line of stubble along his jaw, the close-fitting dark pants that accentuated his lean hips and long legs, the collarless white shirt left unbuttoned at the throat, exposing a deep triangle of smooth, tanned skin…

For a stunned moment she found herself wondering what that skin would feel like under her fingertips—her mouth…

Her mind closed in shock, and she hurried into speech. 'The room is truly lovely. I can't fault your cousin's taste—or her presentation.' She hesitated. 'Although I wonder if it isn't a touch—over-feminine?'

'That is entirely the view of her husband,' Marco acknowledged, his mouth twisting. 'He has stipulated for the new house—no more pink.'

'But it's difficult to know what to suggest without seeing the room in Brussels.' Her brow wrinkled. 'It may face in a different direction…'

'No. Vittoria says it is also south-facing, and very light.'

'In that case…' Flora gave her surroundings another considering look. 'There's a wonderful shade of pale blue-green, called Seascape, that comes in a watered silk paper. I've always felt that waking in sunlight with that on the walls would be like finding yourself floating in the Mediterranean. But your cousin may not want that.'

'On the contrary, I think it would revive for her some happy memories,' Marco returned. 'When we were children we used to stay at my grandfather's house in summer. He had this old *castello* on a cliff above the sea, and we would walk down to the cove each day between the cypress trees.'

'It sounds—idyllic.'

'Yes,' he said quietly. 'A more innocent world.' He paused. 'Have you ever visited my country?'

'Not yet.' Flora lifted her chin. 'But I'm hoping to go there on my honeymoon, if I can persuade my fiancé.'

'He doesn't like Italy?' The green eyes were meditative as they rested on her.

'I don't think he's ever been either. But he was in the Bahamas earlier this year, and that's where he wants to return.' She smiled. 'Apparently there's this tiny unspoiled island called Coconut Cay, where pelicans come to feed. One of the local boatmen takes you there early in the morning with a food hamper and returns at sunset to collect you. Often you have the whole place entirely to yourself.'

There was a silence, then he said expressionlessly, 'It must have happy memories for him.'

'Yes—but I'd rather go to a place where we can create memories together, especially for our honeymoon. We can go to the Bahamas another time.'

'Of course.' He glanced at his watch, clearly bored by her marital plans—which was exactly what she'd intended, she told herself.

'You will make out a written report of your recommendations for Vittoria? With a note of your fee?'

'I'd prefer it if you simply passed on what I've said.' Flora lifted her chin. Met his glance. 'Treat it as cancelling all debts between us.'

'As you wish,' he said courteously.

It wasn't what she'd expected, Flora thought as she trailed downstairs. She'd anticipated some kind of argument, or one of his smiling, edged remarks at the very least.

He'd clearly become bored with whatever game he'd been playing, she told herself, and that had to be all to the good.

She'd intended to continue down the stairs and out of the front door without a backward glance, but Malinda was coming up, carrying an ice bucket, and somehow Flora found herself back in the drawing room.

'Champagne?' Marco removed the cork with swift expertise.

'I really should be going.' Reluctantly she accepted the chilled flute and sat on the edge of a sofa, watching uneasily as the maid adjusted the angle of a plate of canapés on a side table and then withdrew, leaving them alone together. 'Are you celebrating something?'

'Of course. That I am with you again.' He raised his own flute. *'Salute.'*

He was lounging on the arm of the sofa opposite, but she wasn't fooled. He was as relaxed as a coiled spring—or a black panther with its victim in sight...

The bubbles soothed the sudden dryness of her throat. 'Even if you had to trick me into being here?'

'You didn't meet me for dinner the other night.' Marco shrugged. 'What choice did I have?'

'You could have left me in peace,' she said in a low voice.

'There is no peace,' he said with sudden roughness.

'There has not been one hour of one day since our meeting that I have not remembered your eyes—your mouth.'

She said in a stifled tone, 'Please—you mustn't say these things.'

'Why?' he demanded with intensity. 'Because they embarrass—offend you? Or because you have thought of me too, but you don't want to admit it? Which is it, Flora *mia*?'

'You're not being fair…'

'You know the saying,' he said softly. '"All is fair in love and war." And if I have to fight for you, *cara*, I will choose my own weapons.'

'I'm engaged,' she said, with a kind of desperation. 'You know that. I have a life planned, and you have no place in that.'

'So I am barred from your future. So be it. But can you not spare me a few hours from your present—tonight?'

'That—is impossible.'

'You are seeing your *fidanzato* this evening?'

'Yes, of course. We have a great deal to discuss.'

'Naturally,' he said softly. 'And have you told him about me?'

'There was,' she said, steadying her voice, 'nothing to tell.'

He raised his brows. 'He would not be interested to learn that another man knows the taste of his woman—the scent of her skin when she is roused by desire?'

'That's enough.' Flora got up clumsily, spilling champagne on her skirt. 'You have no right to speak to me like this.'

He didn't move, staring at her through half-closed eyes. She felt his gaze touch her mouth like a brand. Scorch through her clothes to her bare flesh.

He said quietly, 'Then give me the right. Have dinner with me tonight.'

'I—can't...' Her voice sounded small and hoarse.

'How strange you are,' he said. 'So confident in your work. Yet so scared to live.'

'That's not true...' The protest sounded weak even in her own ears.

'Then prove it.' The challenge was immediate. 'The day we met I wrote the name of a restaurant on a piece of paper.'

'Which I threw away,' she said, quickly and fiercely.

'But you still remember what it was,' he said gently. 'Don't you, *mia bella*?'

'Why are you doing this to me?' she whispered.

He shrugged. 'I am simply being honest for both of us.' He smiled at her. 'So, tell me the name of the restaurant.'

She swallowed. 'Pietro's—in Gable Street.'

He nodded. 'I shall dine there again this evening. As I told you before, you may join me there at any time after eight o'clock.' He paused. 'And it is just your company at dinner I'm asking for—nothing more. You have my guarantee.'

'You mean you don't...? You won't ask me...?' Flora was floundering.

'No,' Marco Valante said slowly. 'At least—not tonight.'

'Then why...?' She shook her head. 'I don't understand any of this.'

His smile was faint—almost catlike. 'You will find, *mia cara*, that anticipation heightens the appetite. And I want you famished—ravenous.'

She felt the blood burn in her face. She said, 'Then find some other lady to share your feast. Because, as

I've already made clear, I'm not available—tonight or any night.'

All the way to the door she was expecting him to stop her. To feel his hand on her arm—her shoulder. To be drawn back into his embrace.

She gained the stairs. Went down them at a run. Reached the hall where Malinda appeared by magic to open the front door for her and wish her a smiling good evening.

'It's all right,' Flora whispered breathlessly to herself as she crossed the square, heading for the nearest main road to pick up a cab. 'It's over—and you're safe.'

And at that same moment felt a curious prickle of awareness down her spine. Knew that Marco was standing at that first floor window, watching her go.

Yet she not dare to look back and see if she was right. Proving that she wasn't safe at all—and she knew it.

She got the cab to drop her at her neighbourhood supermarket and shopped for the weekend, spending recklessly at the deli counter and wine section.

She needed to get herself centred again, and what better way than a happy weekend with the man she loved, preparing for their future? she asked herself with a touch of defiance.

They could picnic while they worked, she thought, sweetening the pill by buying the things Chris liked best.

As she came round the corner, laden with bags, she saw that his car was parked just down the street from her flat, and felt her heart give a swift, painful thump.

She found him in the living room, sprawled in an armchair, watching a satellite sports channel, but the glance he turned on her was peevish.

'Where on earth have you been? I was expecting you ages ago.'

'I had a job to fit in on the way home, and I shopped.' She held up a bulging carrier. 'See? Goodies.'

'Ah,' he said slowly. 'Actually, I can't stay. That's what I called in to say. Jack Foxton is taking a golf foursome away this weekend and someone's dropped out. So he's asked me to go instead. I've got all my stuff in the car and I'm meeting them at the hotel.'

'Oh, surely not.' Flora stared at him distressfully. 'I had such plans for us.'

'Well, I couldn't turn him down,' he said with a touch of self-righteousness. 'He can put a lot of valuable business my way. You know that. I don't want to upset him.'

Flora lifted her chin. 'Apparently you have no such qualms about upsetting me.'

'Darling.' Belatedly he brought his charm into play. 'It was absolutely a last minute thing, or I'd have let you know earlier. And I'll make it up to you next week. You'll have my undivided attention each evening— promise.'

He got briskly to his feet, tall, blond-haired, blue-eyed and totally single-minded.

Armoured, Flora thought dispassionately, in his own concerns.

She said quietly, 'Chris—don't do this—please. Because I really need to spend some time with you. To talk…'

'And so you shall, sweetheart, when I get back.' He gave her a coaxing smile. 'Anyway, it will give you some space—let you get ahead on the work front—or do some of the girlie things you say you never have time for. Why not give Hester a call? She's probably not doing anything either.'

He aimed a kiss at her unresponsive lips on his way past. 'I'll ring you if I get the chance. If not—see you Monday.'

The door banged, and he was gone.

Flora stood, carriers at her feet, feeling completely deflated and more than a little lost.

Chris was her wall—her barricade against the invasion of all these disturbing thoughts and emotions that were assailing her. And suddenly, frighteningly, he wasn't there for her.

Anger began to stir in her as she recalled his dismissive parting comments. She said aloud, 'How dare he? How bloody *dare* he?'

What low expectations he had of her—and of Hester, come to that, assuming that her friend would have nothing better to do on Friday night than keep her company.

Was that how he had them down? she wondered incredulously. A couple of sad single women settling down with a takeaway and a video? Manless and therefore hapless?

Because, if so, he'd just made the biggest mistake of his life.

She stalked into her bedroom, flung open the wardrobe door and began to search along the hanging rail, pulling out a silky slip of a black dress with shoestring straps and a brief flare of a skirt. She'd bought it a few weeks before and had been waiting for a suitable occasion to wear it.

And tonight was the perfect opportunity, she thought defiantly, removing the price tag and ignoring the alarm signals going off in her brain. That small inner voice telling her that she too was about to commit a blunder that would leave Chris standing. That what she was planning was actually dangerous.

All my life I've played it safe, she argued back, rummaging for the black silk and lace French knickers that were all the dress would accommodate underneath. And where's it got me?

To a situation of being taken totally for granted—that was where.

This wasn't the first time that Chris's business interests had left her stranded at the weekend, she thought. Up to now she'd told herself that his ambition was laudable, that he deserved her whole-hearted support.

But there came a point when ambition became selfishness, and they'd reached it.

Because it wasn't only business which had taken him away from her. He could have cancelled that solo trip to the Bahamas, but he hadn't, even though it had come at a time when she'd desperately needed his love and support. When she hadn't wanted to be left alone.

She hurriedly closed down that train of thought, and the memories it engendered. That was all in the past, and for the moment the future seemed confused. Which left her with the here and now.

And she wasn't going to spend another Friday evening staring at her own four walls when, just for once, there was an attractive alternative.

For a moment she halted, looking at her own startled reflection in her dressing mirror as she acknowledged what she was contemplating. What she was risking.

Because Marco Valante was light years beyond being merely an attractive man. He was a force of nature, she thought, her body shivering in mingled apprehension and excitement.

From the moment she'd seen him that day in the restaurant she'd been drawn to him—a helpless tide to his dark moon.

All that stood between her and potential disaster was his own guarantee that tonight would involve dinner and nothing else. And how did she dare trust a stranger's promise?

Especially when instinct warned her that here was a man who lived by his own rules alone.

She lifted a hand and touched her lips, remembering...

She thought, I must be crazy.

Of course, all she need do was hang the dress back in the wardrobe and spend a blameless evening watching television. No one would be any the wiser.

Yet she already knew in her heart that eminently sensible course of action was not for her.

I'm going to have dinner with him, she thought defiantly. And I'm going to laugh and flirt and have fun in a way I haven't done for months. Just for this one evening. After all, he likes to play games, and I can do that too. And when it's over I'm going to thank him and shake hands nicely, and walk away. Nothing more.

Because I can. Because even if he breaks his word I have my own private armour. It may be called disappointment and failure, but it's very effective just the same. And it confers its own immunity against natural born womanisers like Signor Valante. End of story.

She showered and washed her hair, then finger-dried it so it sprang like an aureole of living flame around her head.

She applied the lightest of make-up, adding a touch of shadow and mascara to her eyes and a pale lustre to her mouth, then slipped her feet into high-heeled strappy sandals.

When she was ready she glanced at herself in the mirror, and gasped. A stranger was looking back at her, her skin milk-white against the starkness of the dress, her face flushed and her eyes bright with expectancy.

And tonight she was going to let that stranger live in her head, she thought, as she sprayed her favourite scent on to pulse-points and picked up her bag and pashmina.

'You still don't have to do this,' she whispered under her breath, as a cab drove her to the restaurant. 'It's not too late. You could always tell the taxi to turn round. But if you go through with it, and it shows any sign of getting heavy, you can leave. So there's nothing—not one thing—to worry about. Whatever happens—you're in control.'

Pietro's was small and quiet, the name displayed on a discreet sign beside the entrance.

Inside, Flora found herself in a smart reception area, confronted by a pretty girl with an enquiring smile.

She cleared her throat. 'I'm meeting someone—a Signor Valante.'

The smile widened. 'Of course, *signorina*. He is in the bar. May I take your wrap?'

'No, it's fine.' Flora maintained a firm grip on its silver-grey folds. 'I'll keep it with me.' In case I have to make a sudden exit, she added silently.

The bar was already busy but she saw him at once, lounging on one of the tall stools at the counter, looking like a man who was prepared to wait all night if he had to.

Only he didn't. Have to. Did he?

Because she was here, and she was trembling again, and that gnawing ache was back in the pit of her stomach.

And of course he had seen her, so it was too late to slip away. In her heart she knew it had always been too late. That something stronger than her own will—her own reason—had brought her to him tonight.

She felt his gaze slide over her. Saw his brows lift and his mouth slant in surprise and frank pleasure as he started towards her through the laughing, chattering groups of people.

And realised, with a pang of something like fear, that, contrary to her expectations—her planned strategy—it would not be as easy as she thought to turn her back and walk away from him when the evening came to an end.

Oh, God, she thought, dry-mouthed. I'm going to have to be careful—so very careful...

CHAPTER THREE

'*CIAO.*' His smile was in his eyes as he reached her side. He took her hand and raised it to his lips in a fleeting caress. 'You decided you could spare me a few hours of your life after all, hmm?'

She took a deep, steadying breath. 'So it would seem,' she returned with relative calm.

'Your *fidanzato* must be a very tolerant man.' His gaze travelled over her without haste, making her feel that he was aware of every detail of what she might— or might not—be wearing. Sending another flurry through her senses.

He said slowly, his lips twisting, 'But I think he would be wiser to keep you chained to his wrist—especially when you look as you do tonight.'

He had not, she realised, relinquished his clasp on her hand, and she detached herself from him, quietly but with emphasis.

'You gave me your word, *signore*, that I would be safe in your company,' she reminded him, trying to speak lightly.

His brows lifted. 'And is that why you came, *mia cara*?' he asked softly. 'Because you wished to feel— safe?'

She gave him a composed smile. 'I came because the food is said to be good here, and I'm hungry.'

'Ah,' he said. 'Then I must feed you.' He made a slight signal and Flora found herself whisked to a small table in the corner—which was somehow miraculously vacant—and supplied with a Campari soda and a menu.

Through an archway she could see tables set with immaculate white cloths and glistening with silverware and crystal, could sniff delectable odours wafting through from the kitchen.

To her own surprise she realised that her flippant remark had been no more than the truth. She was indeed hungry, and the plate of little savoury morsels placed in front of them made her mouth water in sudden greed.

'I am to tell you that my cousin was delighted with your suggestion for her bedroom,' Marco Valante said when they had made their choices from the menu presented by an attentive waiter and were alone again. 'But now, of course, she has asked who makes this particular wall-covering and where it is available.'

'Really?' Flora, who'd been convinced that Vittoria Fairlie's decorating problems were purely fictional, was slightly nonplussed. 'Then I'll send her a full written report with samples next week.'

'She would appreciate it.' He sent her a faint smile. 'It is good of you to take so much trouble.'

'I always take trouble,' she said. She paused. 'Even over commissions that don't really exist.'

He said slowly, 'I wonder if you will ever forgive me for that.'

'Who knows?' She shrugged. 'And why does it matter anyway?' She hesitated again. 'After all, you'll be going back to Italy quite soon—won't you?'

'I have fixed no time for my return.' He smiled at her. 'My plans are—fluid.'

'Your boss must be exceptionally tolerant, in that case.' She heard and hated the primness in her tone.

'We work well together. He does not grudge me a period of relaxation.'

He was silent for a moment, and Flora, conscious that he was studying her, kept her attention fixed firmly on the rosy liquid in her glass. At the same time wondering, in spite of herself, exactly what Marco Valante did for relaxation…

He said, at last, 'So what made you change your mind?'

She gave a slight shrug. 'My—plans didn't work out, that's all.'

'Ah,' he said softly.

She eyed him with suspicion. 'What does that mean?'

'How prickly you are.' His tone was amused. 'Does it have to mean anything?'

She spread her hands almost helplessly. 'How can I tell? I don't seem to know what's going on any more— if I ever did.' She made herself meet his gaze directly. 'And what I really can't figure out is why you're here this evening.'

'Because it's one of my favourite restaurants in London.' The green eyes glinted.

'That isn't what I meant,' Flora said. 'And you know it.' She paused. 'Clearly you know London well, and your cousin lives here and probably leads a hectic social life. I'm sure she could introduce you to dozens of single girls.'

'She has certainly tried on occasion,' he agreed casually.

'Exactly,' Flora said with some force. 'So why aren't you dining with one of them instead?'

He said reflectively, 'Perhaps, *cara*, because I prefer to do my own—hunting.'

She stiffened, eyes flashing. 'I am—not—your prey.'

He grinned unrepentantly. 'No, of course not. Just an angel who has taken pity on my loneliness.'

Her face was still mutinous. 'I'd have said, Signor Valante, that you're the last person in the world who needs to be lonely.'

'*Grazie,*' he said. 'I think.'

'So why, then?' Flora persisted doggedly. 'How is it that you're so set on having dinner with me?'

'You really need to ask?' His brows lifted. 'Are there no mirrors in that apartment of yours?' His voice dropped—became husky. '*Mia bella*, there is not a man in this restaurant who does not envy me and wish he was at your side. How can you not know this?'

Her skin warmed, and she took a hasty sip of her drink. She said stiltedly, 'I wasn't—fishing for compliments.'

'And I was not flattering.' He paused. 'Is the truth so difficult for you to acknowledge?'

She gave a small, wintry smile. 'Perhaps it convinces me that I should have stayed at home.'

'But why?' He leaned forward. Flora thought, crazily, that his eyes were filled with little dancing sparks. 'What possible harm can come to you—in this crowded place?'

She made herself meet his glance steadily. 'I don't know. But I think you're a dangerous man, Signor Valante.'

'You're wrong, *cara*,' he said softly. 'I am the one who is in danger.'

'Then why were you so insistent?'

'Perhaps I like to take risks.'

'Not,' she said, 'a recommendation in an accountant, I'd have thought.'

His grin was lazy. 'But I am only an accountant in

working hours, *carissima*. And now I am not working but relaxing—if you remember.'

Flora bit her lip, conscious of the fierce undertow of his attraction, how it could so easily sweep her out of her depth. If she wasn't careful, of course, she added hastily.

Thankfully, at that moment the waiter reappeared to tell them their table was ready.

And once the food was served, and the wine was poured, she would steer the conversation into more general channels, she promised herself grimly as she accompanied Marco sedately into the main restaurant.

She was faintly ruffled to discover that they were seated side by side on one of the cushioned banquettes. But to request her place to be reset on the opposite side of the table would simply reveal that she was on edge, she reflected as she took her seat.

There was a miniature lamp on the table, its tiny flame bright, but safely confined within its glass shade.

A valuable lesson for life, she thought wryly, as the waiter shook out her napkin and placed it reverently across her lap. She needed to keep the conflict of emotions inside herself controlled with equal strictness.

But she was already too aware of his proximity—the breath of cologne, almost familiar now, that reached her when he moved—the coolly sculptured profile—the dangerous animal strength of the lean body under the civilised trappings. The sensuous curve of the mouth which had once so briefly possessed hers...

This, she was beginning to realise, was a man to whom power was as natural as breathing. And not just material power either, although he clearly had that in plenty, she realised uneasily. His sexual power was even more potent.

She was glad to be able to focus her attention, deservedly, on the food. The delicate and creamy herb risotto was followed by scallops and clams served with black linguine, accompanied by a crisp, fragrant white wine that she decided it would be politic to sip sparingly.

The main course consisted of seared chunks of lamb on the bone, accompanied by a rich assortment of braised garlicky vegetables. The wine was red and full-bodied.

'I'm not surprised you come here,' Flora said after her first appreciative mouthful. 'This food is almost too good.'

He smiled at her. 'I'm glad you approve. But save your compliments for Pietro himself,' he added drily. 'He lives in a state of persistent anxiety and needs all the reassurance he can get.'

'You know him well?'

'We were boys together in Italy.'

'Ah,' she said.

'Now you are being cryptic, *mia bella*,' he said softly. 'What does that mean?'

She shrugged. 'I was just trying to imagine you as a child, with muddy clothes and scraped knees. It isn't easy.'

His brows lifted. 'Do I give the impression I was born in an Armani suit with a briefcase?' he asked lazily.

'Something like that,' she acknowledged, her mouth quirking mischievously.

'Yet I entered the world exactly as you did, Flora *mia*—without clothes at all.' He returned her smile, his eyes flickering lazily over her breasts, clearly outlined by the cling of her dress. 'Shall we indulge in a little— mutual visualisation, perhaps?'

Flora looked quickly down at her plate, aware that her

face had warmed. 'I prefer to concentrate on this wonderful food.'

They ate for a few moments in silence, then Flora ventured into speech again, trying for a neutral topic. 'Italy must be a wonderful country to grow up in.'

'It is also a good place to live when one is grown.' He paused. 'You should introduce me to your *fidanzato*. Maybe I could convince him to take you there.'

Her smile was too swift. Too bright. 'Maybe. But unfortunately he's had to go away this weekend.'

'Another visit to the Bahamas, perhaps?' There was an edge to his voice which she detected and resented.

'No, a business trip,' she returned crisply. 'Chris is his own boss, and that doesn't allow him a great deal of leisure—unlike yourself.'

'Cristoforo,' he said softly. 'Tell me about him.'

'What sort of thing do you want to know?' Flora drank some wine.

'How you met,' he said. 'When you realised that he of all men was the one. But no intimate secrets,' he added silkily. 'That is if you have any to tell...'

Flora bit her lip, refusing to rise to the obvious bait. 'We met at a party,' she said. 'I'd helped a couple sell their flat after it had been on the market almost a year, and they invited me to a housewarming at their new property. Chris was there too because he'd arranged their mortgage. We—started seeing each other and fell in love—obviously. After a few months he proposed to me. And I accepted.'

She saw a faintly derisive expression in his eyes, and stiffened. 'Is there something wrong? Because it seems a perfectly normal chain of events to me.'

'Not a thing,' he said. 'And you will live happily ever after?'

Flora lifted her chin. 'That is the plan, yes.' She paused. 'And what about you, *signore*? Do I get to hear your romantic history—or would it take too long?' She paused. 'Starting, I suppose, with—are you married?'

'No.' His tone was crisp and there was a sudden disturbing hardness in his eyes. 'Nor am I divorced or a widower.' He paused. 'I was once engaged, but it—ended.' He gave her a wintry smile. 'I am sure that does not surprise you.'

'So—you prefer to play the field.' Flora shrugged. 'At least you found out before you were married, so no real harm was done.'

'You are mistaken,' he said slowly. 'It was my *fidanzata* who found another man. Someone she met on holiday.'

'Oh.' This time she was surprised, but tried not to show it. 'Well—these things happen. But they don't usually mean anything.'

Marco Valante gave her a curious look. 'You think it is a trivial matter—such a betrayal?' There was a harsh note in his voice.

'No—no, of course not.' Flora avoided his gaze, her fingers playing uneasily with the stem of her glass. 'I—I didn't mean that. I just thought that if you'd—loved her enough it might have been possible to—forgive her.'

'No.' The dark face was brooding. 'There could be no question of that.'

'Then I'm very sorry,' she said quietly. 'For both of you.' She swallowed. 'It must have been a difficult time. And I—I shouldn't have pried either,' she added. 'Brought back unhappy memories. They say the important thing is to forget the past—and move on.'

'Yes,' he said softly. 'I am sure you are right. But it

is not always that simple. Sometimes the past imposes—obligations that cannot be ignored.'

Flora finished her meal in silence. She felt as if she'd taken an unwary step and found herself in a quagmire, the ground shaking beneath her feet.

There was a totally different side to Marco Valante, she thought. An unsuspected layer of harshness under the indisputable charm. Something disturbingly cold and unforgiving. But perhaps it was understandable. Clearly his fiancée's defection had hit him hard, his masculine pride undoubtedly being dented along with his emotions.

She felt as if she'd opened a door that should have remained closed.

I'll just have some coffee and go, she thought, sneaking a surreptitious glance at her watch.

But that proved not so easy. The waiter, apparently in league with her companion, insisted that she must try the house speciality for dessert—some delectable and impossibly rich chocolate truffles flavoured with amaretto.

And when the tiny cups of espresso arrived they were accompanied by Strega, and also Pietro, the restaurant owner, a small, thin man whose faintly harassed expression relaxed into a pleased grin when Flora lavished sincere praise on his food.

At Marco's invitation he joined them for more coffee and Strega, totally upsetting Flora's plans for a swift, strategic withdrawal.

'I had begun to think we would never meet, *signorina*,' Pietro told her with a twinkle. 'I was expecting you here a few nights ago. You have made my friend Marco wait, I think, and he is not accustomed to that.'

Flora flushed slightly. 'I can believe it,' she said, trying to speak lightly.

'You wrong me, *mia bella*,' Marco Valante drawled. 'I can be—infinitely patient—when it is necessary.'

She felt her colour deepen under the mocking intensity of his gaze. She hurriedly finished the liqueur in her glass, snatched up her bag, and with a murmured apology fled to the powder room.

Thankfully, she had it to herself. She sank down on to the padded stool in front of the vanity unit and stared at herself in the mirror, observing the feverishly bright eyes, the tremulously parted lips, as if they belonged to a stranger.

What in hell was the matter with her? she wondered desperately. She had a career—a life—and a man in that life. And yet she was behaving like a schoolgirl just released from a convent. Only with less sophistication.

And all this because of a man whose existence she'd been unaware of a week ago. It made no sense.

Well, you got yourself into this mess, she reminded herself with grim finality. Of your own free will, too. Even though you should have known better. And now you can just extract yourself—with minimal damage— if that's still possible.

It was hot in the lavishly carpeted, glamorously decorated room, yet Flora was suddenly shivering like a dog.

She felt light-headed too. Maybe she was just sickening for something—one of those odd viruses that kept surfacing in the summer months.

Or maybe she hadn't kept sufficient track, after all, of the number of times Marco Valante had filled and refilled her glass, she thought uneasily.

She'd started off well in control, but had definitely slipped during the course of the long meal—particularly when the conversation had got sticky. She'd tried to use her glass as a barricade, but it might well have turned into a trap instead. And those final Stregas hadn't helped at all.

She smoothed her hair, toned down her hectic cheeks with powder, and rose to her feet.

The dress had been a mistake, too. She'd worn it as a gesture of defiance, but it sent all the wrong messages. And her heels were suddenly far too high as well. They did nothing to combat that dizzy feeling.

She drew a deep breath and held it for a moment before releasing it slowly. Calming tactics before she went back into the restaurant and set about extricating herself from this self-inflicted mess with dignity and aplomb.

'I wish,' she muttered under her breath as she headed for the door, stepping out with more than ordinary care—which was, in itself, a dead giveaway.

She'd been dreading more coffee, more loaded drinks to go with the loaded remarks, but Marco was on his feet, standing by the table, putting away his wallet, his face withdrawn and grave.

It seemed he also wanted to call it a night, thought Flora, summoning relief to her rescue. And perhaps that oddly haunted look had been brought on by the size of the bill...

She paused, angered by her own flippancy when it was undoubtedly her desire to score points by cross-examining him over his love life that had revived too many unwelcome memories and driven him into intro-spection. After all, he was someone who had loved and lost, and in the bitterest circumstances, too, when all she had to do in life was count her blessings.

He glanced up and saw her, and his expression changed. Charm was back in season, and something more than warmth glinted in his eyes. Which she wasn't going to allow herself even to contemplate.

Accordingly, 'Well,' Flora said briskly, when she reached him, 'Thank you for a very pleasant evening, *signore*. And—goodbye.'

'It is not quite over yet,' he corrected her. 'Pietro has called a taxi for us.'

'Oh, he needn't worry about me. I'll be fine.' She reached for her pashmina. 'I'll pick up a black cab...'

'Not easily at this time of night, when the theatres are turning out.' He picked up the long fringed shawl before she could, draping it over his arm. 'And the streets are hardly safe for a woman on her own. I promise you, it would be better to wait.'

Better for whom? Flora wondered, her throat tightening. She stood, gripping her bag, looking down at the tiled floor, until a waiter came to tell them the cab was at the door. She wished Pietro a quiet goodnight, and forced herself to remain passive as Marco placed the pashmina round her shoulders.

Then she walked ahead of him into the street, stumbling a little on an uneven paving stone as the cool night air hit her.

'Take care, *mia bella*. You must not risk another fall.' His hand was under her elbow like a flash, guiding her to the waiting cab.

As she climbed in she heard with shock Marco give the driver her address.

'How do you know where I live?' she demanded, shrinking back into her corner as he took the seat beside her. 'It wasn't on the card I gave you.'

'True.' In the dimness, she saw him lift one shoulder in a shrug. 'But you were not so hard to trace, Flora *mia*.'

'So it would seem,' she said tautly.

It was not that great a distance, but traffic was heavy and the ride seemed to take for ever. Or was it just her acute consciousness of the man in the darkness beside her?

When they finally drew up in the quiet street outside her flat Flora moved swiftly, reaching for the handle. 'Thanks for the lift...'

'You must allow me to see you to your door.' His tone brooked no refusal.

She was concentrating hard on pursuing a steady path across the pavement, at the same time fumbling in her bag for her keys. Not easy when your head was swimming, she thought detachedly, and your legs felt as if all the bones had been removed.

'Let me do this.' There was faint amusement in his voice as he took the key from her wavering hand and fitted it into the lock.

'I can manage,' Flora protested. 'And the taxi's meter will be running,' she added, glancing over her shoulder. She gave an alarmed gasp. 'Oh—it's gone.'

'I hoped you would offer me some coffee.' He was inside now, accompanying her up the stairs, his hand under her arm, supporting her again. Taking it for granted, she thought furiously, that it was necessary. 'Isn't that the conventional thing to do?' he added.

'You wouldn't know a convention, Signor Valante, if it jumped out and bit you.' Not all her words were as clear as she'd have liked, but she thought she'd got the meaning across.

'On the other hand, I could make *you* some coffee,' he went on. 'You seem to need it.'

'I'm perfectly fine,' Flora returned with dignified imprecision. 'And our dinner date is over, in case you hadn't noticed.'

'Yes,' he said. 'But the evening still goes on. And I am curious to see where you live.'

'Why?' She watched him fit the flat key in the lock.

He shrugged. 'Because you can learn a great deal from someone's surroundings. You of all people should know that,' he added drily. 'And there are things I wish to discover about you.'

She gave him a brilliant smile. 'Good luck,' she said, and led the way into the living room.

Marco Valante halted, looking slowly round him, taking in the plain white walls, the stripped floorboards, the low glass-topped table, and the sofa and single armchair in their tailored smoky blue covers.

He said softly, 'A blank canvas. How interesting. And is the bedroom equally neutral?'

Flora walked back across the narrow passage and flung open the door opposite. 'Judge for yourself,' she said, and watched his reaction.

Here, there were no touches of colour at all. Everything from the walls to the fitted wardrobes which hid her clothes, and the antique lace bedcover and the filmy drapes that hung at the window, was an unremitting white.

'Very virginal,' Marco said after a pause, his face expressionless. 'Like the cell of a nun. It explains a great deal.'

'Such as?' she demanded.

'Why your *fidanzato* prefers to spend his time elsewhere, perhaps.'

'As it happens, Chris is here all the time. And he likes a—a minimalist look,' she flung back at him. 'And now that you've seen what you came for, you can leave.'

'Without my coffee?' He shook his head reproachfully. 'You are not very hospitable, Flora *mia.*'

She said between her teeth, 'Please stop calling me "your" Flora.'

'You wish me to call you "his" Flora—this Cristoforo's—when it is quite clear you do not belong to him—and never have?'

She might not be firing on all cylinders, but she could recognise disdain when she heard it.

'You know nothing about my relationship with my fiancé,' she threw back at him, discomfited to hear her words slurring. 'And you're hardly the person to lecture me on how to conduct my engagement. I think it's time you went.'

'And I think you're more in need of coffee than I am, *signorina.*' He walked down the passage to the kitchen. Flora, setting off in pursuit with a gasp of indignation, arrived in time to see him filling the kettle and setting it to boil.

'You have no espresso machine?' He glanced round at her, brows lifted.

'No,' Flora said with heavy sarcasm. 'I'm sorry, but I didn't realise I'd be entertaining an uninvited guest.'

'If you think you are in the least entertaining, you delude yourself.' He reached for the cafetière. 'Where do you keep your coffee?'

Mute with temper, she opened a cupboard and took down a new pack of a freshly ground Colombian blend.

She said curtly, 'I'll do it.'

'As you wish.' He shrugged, and took her place in the doorway, leaning a casual shoulder against its frame.

'You give little away,' he remarked after a pause. 'No pictures—no ornaments or personal touches. You are an enigma, Signorina Flora. A woman of mystery. What are you trying to conceal, I wonder?'

'Nothing at all,' Flora denied, spooning coffee into the cafetière. 'But I work with colour all the time. When I get home I prefer something—more restful, that's all.'

'Is that the whole truth?'

She bit her lip, avoiding his quizzical gaze. 'Well, I did plan to decorate at first—perhaps—but then I met Chris, so now I'm saving my energies for the home we're going to share. That's going to be a riot of colour. The showcase for my career.'

'You say you plan to go on working after you are married?'

Flora lifted her chin. 'Naturally. Is something wrong with that?'

'You do not intend to have babies?'

She began to set a tray with cups, sugar bowl and cream jug. 'Yes—probably—eventually.'

'You do not sound too certain.'

She opened the cutlery drawer with a rattle to look for spoons. 'Maybe I feel I should get the wedding over with before I start organising the nursery.'

'Do you like children?'

'Boiled or fried?' Flora filled the cafetière and set it on the tray. 'I don't know a great deal about them, apart from my sort of nephew, and he's a nightmare—spoiled rotten and badly behaved. A real tantrum king.'

'Perhaps you should blame the parents rather than the child.'

'I do,' she said shortly. 'Each time I'm forced to set eyes on him.' She picked up the tray and turned, noting that he was still blocking the doorway. 'Excuse me—please.'

He made no attempt to move, and she added, her tone sharpening, 'I—I'd like to get past.'

'Truly?' he asked softly. 'I wonder.' He straightened and took the tray from her suddenly nerveless hands.

Taking a breath, Flora marched ahead of him back to the sitting room, deliberately choosing the armchair.

He placed the tray on the glass table and sat down on the sofa. 'I am beginning to accustom myself to your unsullied environment.' His tone was silky. 'But I find it odd that there are no photographs anywhere—none of your Cristoforo—or of your parents either. Are you an orphan, perhaps? Is your past as unrevealing as your walls?'

'Of course not,' she said coolly. 'I have plenty of family pictures, but I keep them in an album. I don't like—clutter.'

His brows lifted mockingly. 'Is that how you regard the image of your beloved?'

'No, of course not.' She bit her lip. 'You like to deliberately misunderstand.'

'On the contrary, I am trying to make sense of it all.' He paused. 'Of you.'

'Then please don't bother,' Flora said swiftly. 'Our acquaintance has been brief, and it ends tonight.'

'Ah,' he said softly. 'But the night is not yet over. So I am permitted a little speculation.'

'If you want to waste your time.' Flora reached for the cafetière and filled the cups, controlling a little flurry of unease.

'My time is my own. I can spend it as I wish.' He paused. 'So—are you going to show me these photographs of yours—if only to prove they really exist?'

For a moment she hesitated, then reluctantly opened

the door of one of the concealed cupboards beside the fireplace and extracted a heavy album.

She took it across to him and held it out. 'Here. I have nothing to hide.' She gave him a taut smile. 'My whole history in a big black book.'

He opened the album and began to turn the pages, his face expressionless as he studied the pictures.

Flora picked up her coffee cup and sipped with apparent unconcern.

He said, 'Your parents are alive and in good health?'

She paused, chewing her lip again. 'My father died several years ago,' she said at last. 'And my mother remarried—a widower with a daughter about my own age.'

'Ah,' he said softly. 'The mother of the tantrum king. Is that why you don't like her?'

'I have no reason to dislike her,' Flora said evenly. 'We haven't a great deal in common, that's all.'

He turned another page and paused, the green eyes narrowing. He said, 'And this, of course, must be Cristoforo. How strange.'

She stiffened. 'Why do you say that?'

'Because he is the only man to feature here.' His voice was level. 'Were there no previous men in your life, Flora *mia*? No minor indiscretions of any kind? Or have they been whitewashed away too?'

'I've had other boyfriends,' she said coldly. 'But no one who mattered. All right?'

He looked down again at the photograph, his mouth twisting. 'And he means the world to you—as you do to him?'

'Of course. Why do you keep asking me all these questions.'

'Because I want to know all about you, *mia cara*. Every last thing.'

Her throat tightened. 'But no one can ever know another person that well.'

'Then perhaps I shall be the first.' He closed the photograph album and laid it aside. He rose, taking off his jacket and tossing it across the back of the sofa, then walked across to her, taking her hands in his and pulling her to her feet. She went unresistingly, her heart beating a frantic, alarmed tattoo, her eyes widening in a mixture of panic and strange excitement.

He said softly, 'And I shall start with your mouth.'

'No,' Flora said hoarsely as his arms went round her, drawing her against the hard heat of his body. 'You can't. You said—you promised—that I'd be safe tonight.'

'And so you have been, *mia bella*.' There was laughter in his voice, mingled with another note, more dangerous, more insidious. 'But midnight has come and gone. It is no longer tonight, but tomorrow. And from this moment on I guarantee nothing.'

He added softly, 'You can command me not to touch you, but not to stop wanting you. Because that has become impossible.'

Then he bent his head, and his lips met hers.

CHAPTER FOUR

SOME distant voice in her mind was telling her that she should fight him. That she should kick, bite and punch, if necessary, before the warmth of his mouth on hers sapped every last scrap of resistance from her being.

That she should hang on, with every ounce of will she possessed, to her life—her safe, planned future with Chris.

And to her reason—her sanity.

But it was too late. Indeed, she realised helplessly, it had always been too late—from that first time she had seen him in the restaurant. And, even more, from that fleeting moment when his lips had first touched hers.

It was pointless to remind herself that she had no moral right to be doing this. That she was engaged—committed—soon to be married. That this was a madness she could not afford. Because logic, reason, even decency no longer seemed to matter.

And the most shaming thing of all was that he was using no force—because he didn't have to. Because her lips were already parting in acceptance, and welcome. And with a growing hunger she was no longer able to disguise, even had she wanted to.

Her mind—her will—was in free fall—cascading into surrender.

And the hands which had been braced in the beginnings of protest against the wall of his chest lifted and locked at the nape of his neck.

At first it was a gentle, almost leisurely exploration of

her mouth, as if he was learning the taste—the texture of her. Then, slowly, the kiss deepened, imposing new demands. Testing the outer limits of her control. And his.

Her body was pressed against him, making her aware that he was powerfully aroused. The hurry of his heartbeat seemed translated into her own being.

He pushed a hand into her hair, twining the silky strands round his fingers, drawing her head backwards so that the long, lovely line of her throat was exposed and vulnerable to the lingering passage of his caress. His lips found the pink shell of her ear, then travelled down to the frantic tumult of her pulse.

She gasped as she felt the heated, animal surge in her blood. As his lips encountered the delicate hollows at the base of her throat, pushing aside the narrow strap, baring the curve of her shoulder.

The long fingers found the rounded curve of her breast, moulding it gently as his thumb moved delicately, voluptuously on the hardening nipple. Flora leaned her forehead against his shoulder, eyes closed, lost in exquisite shuddering sensation.

Whatever coherency remained in her mind told her that she had never felt like this before. Never dreamed it was possible that she could *want* like this. That she could welcome every new intimacy and long for more.

She heard herself say hoarsely, 'What do you want from me?'

'Everything.' His voice was a husky whisper, the single word an affirmation. Almost a warning.

He kissed her again with slow, sensual purpose, while his hands continued their absorbed, teasing play with the heated peaks of her breasts, making her sigh her pleasure against his lips.

She wasn't even sure when he released the zip at the back of her dress, letting the soft fabric slide away from her shivering skin.

He lifted her into his arms, sinking back with her on to the sofa, holding her so that she was lying across his thighs, the black dress pooling round her hips, her entire body attuned—accessible—to the touch of his hands and mouth.

She heard him murmur in throaty appreciation as his dark head bent to adore the scented mounds he had uncovered, and she quivered as she felt the burn of his lips against her skin—the flickering glide of his tongue on her nipples.

She made a little stifled sound and he lifted his head, looking down at her, the green eyes warm and slumbrous.

'You don't like that?'

'Oh, yes,' she whispered. 'Too much—too much.'

He stroked each taut peak with a gentle finger. 'They are like tiny roses,' he told her softly. 'Only more sweet.'

Her own hands were pulling feverishly at the buttons on his shirt to free them, touch the heated, hairroughened skin beneath, and he helped her, dragging the loosened edges apart, then lifting her triumphantly, almost fiercely, so that her naked breasts grazed his own.

His mouth closed on hers with renewed fire, and she clung to him, half dizzy with abandonment, aware of nothing but the pagan clamour of her flesh.

He moved suddenly, lifting her away from him, setting her on her feet, and for an instant she looked at him in mute bewilderment. He smiled slowly up at her, letting his hands drift down her body to disentangle her finally from the ruin of her dress.

When it was done Marco stared at her for a long moment, absorbing the contrast between the creaminess of her skin and the silken black of the tiny undergarment which was her sole remaining covering.

He said softly, 'All evening I have been imagining how you would look at this moment, and you are more beautiful than any fantasy, Flora *mia*.'

His fingers spanned her waist lightly. 'Because you are real.'

His touch lingered on her flat stomach. 'And warm.'

His hand moved downward, brushing over the fragile silk, until he reached the scalding secret core of her, where he lingered.

'And wanting me,' he added huskily.

With one lithe movement he was on his feet, lifting her effortlessly into his arms and walking with her out of the room, and across the passage into the stark whiteness of her bedroom.

Still holding her, he bent slightly, switching on the lamp beside the bed, then took hold of the immaculate bedspread, pulling it back and tossing it to the foot of the bed before lowering Flora to the mattress.

She looked up at him through half-closed eyes as he stood over her. She was aware of the thud of her heart, the rapid rise and fall of her breasts as sudden nervousness lent an edge to her excitement. And she was conscious too that it was a stranger's face that looked down at her in the lamplight, shadowed and almost feral in its intensity.

Her throat tightened. 'Is something—wrong?'

'Nothing.' The sound of her voice seemed to awake him from some spell. His smile banished the shadow— or had that just been a figment of her overwrought imagination? 'Except that you are still wearing too many clothes, *mia bella*.'

'So,' she whispered, 'are you.'

'You think so?' He gave a soft laugh. 'Well, that is easily remedied.'

He stripped with deftness and grace, and without apparent self-consciousness, although she knew he was watching her watch him.

Watching her widening eyes, and the swift, betraying flush that stained her cheeks as she absorbed his lean, strong, totally masculine beauty. The flutter of the muscles in her suddenly dry throat, as apprehension took hold. As she remembered…

Her eyes and her mind went blank. She wanted to run—to hide—to be a thousand miles from this place—this room—this bed—where pain and humiliation waited for her all over again.

The flame in her veins was cooling to ice. The swift, mindless rapture that had consumed her such a short time ago had burned itself out, leaving her with only the ashes.

She thought, Oh, God—what can I do? What can I say…?

She felt the bed dip as he came to lie beside her. Heard him say her name with a question in his voice.

Fingers as gentle as the brush of a feather stroked her hot cheek, then inexorably turned her face towards him.

He said quietly, 'Tell me.'

Pointless to pretend she didn't understand.

She said, falteringly, 'I'm not a virgin—at least, not completely.'

She'd been afraid he would laugh, or be scornful, but instead he nodded, the green eyes thoughtful.

'You are telling me that you have made love with your *fidanzato* after all?'

'Not—exactly.' She swallowed. 'This is—so difficult to explain.'

'No,' Marco said. 'You forget—I have seen your eyes, *mia bella*. And I do not believe that your first surrender was a happy experience for you. Is that what you are trying to say?'

'Yes—I suppose.' She flushed unhappily, avoiding his gaze. 'But it wasn't Chris's fault. I just didn't realise it would—hurt so much.'

She tried to smile. 'It's so ridiculous. I'm a twenty-first century woman, not some early Victorian. It never occurred to me...' Her voice trailed into silence.

He stroked her hair back from her forehead. 'And when the pain was over, did he give you pleasure?'

He sounded totally matter-of-fact—as if he was asking if she thought it would rain tomorrow, she told herself, bewildered.

She said stiltedly, 'He was very—kind about it. But, naturally, he was terribly upset that he'd hurt me. So he suggested it might be better—to wait—before trying again. So we—have...'

'Such amazing self-control.' The cool drawl held a sudden bite. 'I am filled with admiration.'

'He was thinking of me,' Flora defended swiftly.

He shrugged a negligent shoulder. 'Did I suggest otherwise?'

'And it was my problem—my failure,' she went on with determination.

'With lovers, there is no question of failure,' he said softly. 'Some times are better than others—that is all.' He paused. 'As for this problem you believe you have—we shall solve it together.'

Her voice shook. 'I don't think—I can...'

'Ah,' he said. 'But you will. And that is a promise, Flora *mia*. So, do you believe me? Say, ''Yes, Marco.'''

A tiny shaken laugh escaped her. 'Yes, Marco.'

'Then why are you still trembling?'

She thought, Because no matter how scared I might be, you make me tremble—and burn—and shiver—and ache. And even if I had all the experience in the world you would still possess the power to do this to me. Because—with you—I cannot help myself.

She said, with a catch in her voice, 'I think you know…'

He said quietly, 'Perhaps.'

He framed her face in his hands and began to kiss her again, lightly and sensuously, making no further demands until her taut body began gradually to relax and her lips parted for him on a little sigh of acceptance. His kiss deepened, showing her a glimpse of hunger held well in check. Leaving her almost disappointed when he took his mouth from hers.

He held her for a long time, murmuring to her in his own language, his long fingers stroking her tumbled hair, her cheek, the line of her throat, his gentleness a reassurance. And a seduction.

When his lips next touched hers Flora responded like a flower turning to the sun, offering her mouth's inner sweetness without restraint.

As they kissed Marco began to caress her, the experienced hands slowly rediscovering the curves and planes of her body, revealing them to her anew through his touch.

She had never known there could be such excitement in the brush of skin on skin. She was warming deliciously, her body tinglingly alive to the subtle caress of his fingers, so intent on every new sensation he was offering that she hardly knew the moment when he slipped off her final covering and she was naked in his arms at last.

When his hand parted her thighs, her little gasp was lost under the answering pressure of his lips, as he kissed her deeply and with mounting sensuality. And any sense of shock or shyness was drowned in the flood of sensation which instantly assailed her.

His fingers stroked and tantalised, demanding her quivering body to yield up its most intimate secrets to him. Turning her slowly and deliberately to liquid fire.

She began to move in response to his caress, her body arching tautly towards him as his lips returned to her breasts, suckling the rosy peaks with voluptuous delight. At the same time his exploring hand discovered, then focused on another tiny hidden mound, moving gently and rhythmically on its moist, silken pinnacle.

She was making small helpless sounds in her throat, her head twisting involuntarily on the pillow. She was dissolving in pleasure, her attention absorbed, blindly concentrated on the delicate arousing play of his fingertips with an intensity that bordered on pain. Nothing existed but this man and what he was doing to her, she thought, as her breathing changed and even this last contact with reality slid away.

Even so, the final dark waves of ecstasy caught her unawares, lifting her to a sphere she had never known existed and holding her there, suspended in some rapturous vacuum, while she called out in a voice she didn't recognise and her body shattered into the uncontrollable spasms of her first climax.

She descended slowly, every inch of her body throbbing with a new languor yet feeling alive as never before.

She lifted heavy eyelids and looked up at her lover, and her hand went up to touch his face, feeling the taut jaw muscles clench under her fingers. He captured her questioning fingers and carried them to his lips, biting the tips gently.

She said softly, huskily, 'Is it appropriate to say thank you?'

'If you wish.' There was a smile in his voice, and his mouth was curving in disturbingly sensual appreciation.

Flora realised suddenly that he was moving—positioning himself over her without haste but with definite purpose. 'But I would prefer a more—tangible demonstration, *mia cara*,' he added softly, easing his way into her newly slackened and totally receptive body.

She looked up at him, her eyes wide and startled as she felt herself filled—possessed utterly.

'Hold me,' he instructed tautly, and she obeyed, her hands clinging to the smooth brown shoulders as he began to thrust into her, gently at first, his eyes watching hers for any sign of fear or reluctance, and then more powerfully—more urgently.

She had thought that he had taken her to the extremes of sensation, and beyond. That she was sated—content to be passive while he took his own satisfaction.

But, as she soon discovered with astonishment, she was wrong. Because her body was answering him—mirroring the strong, controlled rhythm of his lovemaking.

She lifted her legs, wrapping them round his sweat-dampened body, and he slid his hands beneath her, raising her towards him as he found her mouth with his.

His kiss was raw and passionate, and her surrender was total, dominated by the renewed demands of her own fevered flesh.

The rasp of his breathing was echoed by her own. She

felt as if she was poised on the edge of some abyss, and he must have felt it too, because he spoke to her, his voice hoarse and urgent. 'Come for me, *mia bella—mia cara*. Come now.'

And, deep within her, as if answering his cue, Flora felt the first sharp pulsation of rapture. She moaned aloud, burying her face against him, biting his shoulder, as the moment took her and sent her spinning out of control into some limbo where pleasure bordered on pain.

Marco flung his head back, his eyes closed, his face taut with the same kind of agony, and she felt his entire body shudder like a tree caught in a giant wind as he came in his turn.

When it was over, they lay together quietly. Flora tried to steady her breathing, to make sense of what had happened to her.

'I didn't know.' Her voice was a thread. He didn't answer, and she turned her head to look at him. He was lying, staring up at the ceiling, his profile as proud and remote as a Renaissance carving.

She felt her throat tighten. 'Marco—is something wrong?'

He turned his head slowly, and smiled at her. 'What could possibly be wrong, Flora *mia*?'

'You looked a thousand miles away.'

He shrugged a shoulder. 'I was thinking how ironic it is that I should have come all this way to find my perfect woman.'

'Truly?'

'You doubt me?'

'No,' she said slowly. 'It's just—that was a happy thought, and you didn't look very happy.'

'And you, *mia bella*, look as if you need to stop imagining things and sleep.' He gathered her closer, so that her head was pillowed on his chest. She could feel the beat of his heart, still slightly uneven, under her cheek.

He was not, she thought with satisfaction, as cool as he seemed. And she closed her eyes, smiling.

She slept deeply and dreamlessly, and awoke with reluctance. For a moment she lay still, feeling oddly disorientated—as if her faintly aching body no longer belonged to her. And then, like a thunderbolt, her memory returned and she sat up.

Oh, God, she thought desperately. I'm in bed with Marco Valante.

Except that wasn't strictly true. Because no sleeping man lay beside her. Nor, she realised, was there any sound from the bathroom, or any sign of his clothes either.

She said aloud, 'He's gone.' And her voice sounded small and desolate in the emptiness of the room.

She lay down again, pulling the tangled sheet up over her body, aware that her mouth was dry and her heart was thumping.

Well, Flora, she told herself. It seems you've just had your first one-night stand. Now you have to live with that, and I just hope you think it was worth it.

And, to make matters a million times worse, you've had unprotected sex with a stranger. A man who's probably left his notch on bedposts in every major capital of the world, and several small towns as well. And that's something else you'll have to deal with.

She pressed her clenched fist against her mouth, to stop herself from moaning aloud.

She had no one to blame but herself, whatever the consequences. After all, she'd gone out last night undressed to kill, flinging down a challenge to his sexuality that no red-blooded man could have ignored. And all because of a fit of pique.

She stopped right there. Because that was too easy—too glib an excuse for what she had done.

From that first glimpse of him, Marco had intrigued her. Had tantalised his way into her dreams, sleeping and waking. He himself had been the challenge—and the ultimate prize.

And she had hardly been short-changed. In a few brief hours Marco had taught her more about her body and its needs than she could have believed possible.

And she would never be the same again.

The girl who had had the rest of her life mapped out, with a sensible marriage and a secure future, had disappeared for ever—if she'd even existed at all.

What was it Hester had said? 'Heaven, hell and heartbreak'?

Well, she'd had the heaven, and now she was faced with the hell of knowing that, for him, it had been just a casual sexual encounter—another girl in another bed. And, although she was currently feeling numb, she knew the heartbreak would surely follow.

And then there was Chris, whom she had betrayed in the worst possible way.

I can't tell him, she thought miserably. I can't hurt him like that. He doesn't deserve it. I'll have to find some other excuse for calling off the wedding. Tell him I've been having second thoughts—that I prefer my career—my independence.

His mother will be pleased, anyway. She never thought I was good enough for him—always dropping hints about modern girls not knowing how to be homemakers.

She groaned, pressing her face into the pillow. No amount of self-justification was ever going to excuse what she'd done. She'd had no right to have dinner with Marco Valante, let alone allow him to make a feast of her in bed.

And now he'd walked away without a backward glance, and she knew she had no one to blame but herself.

Act like a tart and you'll get treated like a tart, she thought drearily.

She pushed away the encircling sheet and got up. It was the morning after the night before, and she simply had to get on with her life. She would have a bath—wash away the taste and touch of Marco Valante—get dressed, then start to dismantle the arrangements for the wedding that were already in place. Florists, caterers and printers would all have to be notified, and the church cancelled. She would need to make a list, she thought, trailing into the bathroom and turning on the taps in the tub.

And somehow she would have to tell her mother, and endure the inevitable wailings and recriminations.

On the plus side, she thought wanly, I will not have the nephew from hell following me up the aisle, although I expect that Sandra will have something to say about her little darling's disappointment.

She poured a capful of her favourite bath essence into the steaming water.

There was going to be a lot of music to face, she thought frowningly, but only if she chose to do so. She could always take the weeks she'd booked off for her honeymoon and move them up. Get right away for a while and put herself back together again.

Some of the clients she'd planned to see might not be

too happy if she went missing for a couple of weeks, but Melanie would simply have to make new appointments for them.

It'll be good for her, she thought, testing the water. Show what she's made of in a crisis.

And she was ready to bet that most of the clients would be prepared to wait for her return. Because she was good at her job.

I wish, she thought, as she stepped into the tub, that I was equally as good at life.

She settled back into the scented water with a little sigh and closed her eyes.

She'd made a monumental fool of herself, and taken a terrible risk, but she didn't have to allow it to cloud her entire future, she told herself firmly. Everyone was surely allowed one serious mistake—and Marco Valante was hers. That was all.

She heard a slight sound, and turned her head sharply.

Her serious mistake was standing in the bathroom doorway, one shoulder negligently propped against its frame. He was fully dressed, but tieless, and his shirt was open at the throat.

He said softly, *'Buon giorno.'* And began to walk towards her, discarding his jacket as he did so. 'I thought you would sleep until my return, *cara.*'

'Your return?' Her voice was a stifled croak. 'Where have you been?'

'Your refrigerator was full of food, but nothing for breakfast, so I went shopping.' He counted on his fingers. 'We have fresh rolls, orange juice, cheese and some good ham.' The green eyes glinted as they surveyed her. 'All of which we will have—later.'

Flora realised he was rolling up the sleeves of his

shirt. He reached down and took the soap from her un-resisting hand.

'Stand up, *mia bella*,' he directed quietly.

Somehow she found herself mutely obeying, her eyes fixed on his face, aware that her throat had tightened with mingled panic and excitement.

Marco lathered his hands with the soap and began to apply the scented foam to her skin, starting with her shoulders and working his way downwards, massaging it into her body very slowly, and very thoroughly.

His gaze was reflective—almost dispassionate—as he worked—like a sculptor judging his latest work, she thought confusedly as her senses began to riot.

Everywhere he touched her—and he didn't seem to miss an inch—was tingling and burning. An agonised trembling had ignited deep inside her.

Her breasts were aching with desire as his fingers lingered over their rosy tips. She quivered as he moved with exquisite precision down the length of her spine to her rounded buttocks.

When he touched her thighs, and the soft curls at their apex, Flora had to bite her lower lip to prevent herself from whimpering out loud.

When he'd finished, he took the hand spray from the shower unit and rinsed away the soap, just as carefully. The water droplets felt like needles piercing her over-sensitised skin as they cascaded over her small round breasts, making the nipples stand proud.

At last, when she was beginning to think she could bear no more, he turned off the spray and reached to the towel rail for a bath sheet. He took her hand and helped her out of the water, then wrapped the soft towelling round her.

'Dry yourself, *carissima*,' he ordered softly. 'I would not wish you to catch a chill.'

Chill? Flora thought, as she started, dazedly, to pat herself dry under his unwavering scrutiny. She was already running a high fever. Her legs were shaking so much that she thought she might collapse and her blood was on fire. And he had to know this.

When she had finished, she paused, her eyes asking a question. He nodded, as if she had spoken aloud. He took the edges of the bath sheet, using them to pull her gently towards him. His arms enfolded her and his mouth came down on hers in a slow, deep kiss that sent her already reeling senses into free fall.

When he raised his head, his own breathing was ragged. He drew the edges of the bath sheet apart and began to kiss her body, his lips drifting soft as thistledown from her throat down to her breasts, then travelling over her ribcage to the faint concavity of her abdomen.

He sank down on one knee, his hands holding her hips as the trail of kisses continued downward. When he reached the division of her thighs, and parted them, she gave a little startled cry as she felt his mouth on the burning core of her, the silken eroticism of his tongue as he pleasured her tiny secret bud.

She wanted to tell him that he must not do this—that he should stop. But she could not speak.

She was conscious of nothing but the exquisite sensations rippling through her as he continued his intimate caress. Every atom of her being was focused almost painfully on her growing delight. And then, almost before she was aware, her body imploded into orgasm, the pulsations so strong she thought she might faint.

There were tears running down her face. He wiped

them away with the edge of the towel, then picked her up in his arms and carried her towards the door.

'Where are we going?' Her voice was a breathless squeak.

'Back to bed.'

'But we were going to have breakfast.'

'I think now that is going to be—very much later.' He bent and kissed her mouth, fiercely, sensually. 'Don't you agree, *mia cara*?'

Flora pressed her lips against the triangle of hair-darkened skin revealed by his unfastened shirt. 'Yes, Marco.' Her voice was husky. 'Oh—yes—please.'

CHAPTER FIVE

A LONG time later, lying in his arms, Flora said dreamily, 'I think we've missed breakfast—but it could always become lunch.'

Marco tipped up her chin and looked down at her, brows raised austerely. 'You mean I am not enough for you? You want food as well?'

She gave a soft giggle. 'I think I need to keep my strength up—if this is how you mean us to spend our time.'

She felt the arm that encircled her harden with sudden tension, and realised, with shock, that she'd spoken as if they had a real relationship. That she'd made unwise assumptions about a future which almost certainly did not exist.

She turned away quickly as her face warmed in helpless embarrassment. 'Anyway—I—I'll get us something to eat...' she added with determined brightness.

She pushed away the covering sheet, then hesitated as she remembered that her robe was in the bathroom.

It was ludicrous, she thought with bewilderment. This was the man with whom she'd been intimately entwined for the best part of twelve hours, who had explored and kissed every inch of her body, and yet, in the space of a drawn breath, everything had changed. And suddenly she was reluctant to walk around naked in front of him.

Lack of inhibition was different when it was fuelled by passion. She'd given herself to him again and again in unthinking delight. Learned to bestow pleasure as well as receive it.

But now reason had intervened.

And it was still nothing more than a one-night stand, no matter how she might try to justify it. There'd been no commitment of any kind between them. It had been— just sex. A transient pleasure. And now the sex was over she felt awkward and bewildered—unsure how to behave.

Because Marco, in so many ways, was still a stranger to her, she acknowledged unhappily. Someone who had walked into her life a few days ago and who would soon be leaving in the same casual way.

And it was naïve of her to have supposed—or hoped—that anything that had happened had any real importance in the great scheme of things.

As a lover Marco was gifted, patient and imaginative, luring her into areas of sensuousness she had not know existed.

But she knew that no amount of pleasure would ever be matched by the pain of watching him leave.

It's so easy for a man, she thought sadly. He can just get dressed and go. Whereas I—I've slept with Marco once, and now I want to make him a meal. Next I'll be wanting to have his baby.

Behind her, Marco moved. 'Is something wrong?' He brushed his lips gently across the small of her back. 'You are not having—regrets?'

'No—of course not.' She spoke bravely, not looking at him. 'I was just wondering—where I'd left my dressing gown.'

She heard the smile in his voice. 'Does that really matter?'

She said shortly, 'It does to me.'

There was a silence, then he said slowly, '*Cara*, are you trying to tell me you are—shy?'

She bit her lip. 'Is that so extraordinary?'

He said, 'A little, perhaps, considering what you and I were doing to each other a little while ago.' He paused. 'Would it make things easier for you if I promised to shut my eyes?'

'Yes,' she agreed with a touch of defiance. 'Yes, it would.'

He sighed. 'Just for you, then, *mia bella*.'

Flora slipped out of bed and made for the door. As she reached it something prompted her to look back over her shoulder.

Marco was propped up on an elbow, watching her with undisguised and shameless appreciation.

'Oh,' she choked furiously, and flew to the bathroom, followed by his laughter.

By the time she had prepared lunch, adding fresh fruit and a dish of black olives to the food he'd provided, and choosing a bottle of wine, she was feeling altogether more composed.

While he'd been in the bathroom she'd snatched the opportunity to dress, in a brief blue skirt and white tee shirt, and give her hair a vigorous brushing.

She looked different, she realised with a sense of shock as she glanced at herself in the mirror. There was a new glow to her creamy skin, a woman's shining secrets in her eyes. She was no longer the innocent of twenty-four hours ago, and everything about her proclaimed it.

All she needed to do now was develop a persona to go with her new-found sexual sophistication, she thought wryly. Find something hip and flippant to accompany her smile when she waved Marco goodbye. Proving beyond doubt, she hoped, that she'd always known this was a strictly casual encounter.

When she was alone she ate at the breakfast bar in the kitchen, but for guests she kept a folding table in the walk-in cupboard in the hall. She'd set this up in the corner of the living room, with the directors' chairs which accompanied it.

She was just opening the wine when Marco came to the door.

'*Bello,*' he approved softly. 'A feast.' He indicated the towel draped decorously round his hips. 'See, I am sparing your blushes, *cara.*'

Flora bit her lip. 'You must think I'm awfully stupid…'

'You are wrong. I find you a delight.' He held out a hand. 'Come to me.'

She went over to him and he drew her close, resting his cheek against the top of her head while she inhaled the clean, fresh scent of his skin.

After a moment she stood back, studying a discoloured mark on his shoulder. 'What's that?'

He grinned at her. 'Don't you remember?'

'Oh,' she said, discomfited. 'I—I'm sorry.'

'Then don't be. I like my battle trophy—and its memories.'

'Is that how you see making love—as a war?' She laughed, but she felt faintly troubled too. 'Then who is the victor and who the vanquished?'

He kissed her, his mouth moving on hers with tender warmth. 'At a moment like this,' he murmured, 'it hardly seems to matter.' He paused, stroking the hair back from her face. 'And don't look at me like that, Flora *mia,*' he added softly. 'Or lunch might become dinner.'

Her glance didn't waver. 'I wouldn't mind.'

'Then let me be wise for us both.' His smile was rueful. 'I think it is time I also put on some clothes.'

He kissed her again, and went soft-footed back to the bedroom.

It was a quiet lunch. Marco seemed lost in thought more than once. Or perhaps, thought Flora, he was just exhausted...

'What are you thinking?' he asked.

'Nothing in particular.' She took a hasty swig of wine. 'Why?'

'Because you are blushing again. I thought it might be—significant.'

'Not really.' Flora fanned herself with her napkin. 'It's probably the heat. It's such a beautiful day.' She paused. 'Would you like some more wine?'

'No, I thank you.' He glanced at his watch. 'I must get back to my cousin's house. And I shall be driving later.'

Oh, Flora thought flatly. So—that was that, after all. And she couldn't pretend it was a surprise.

'It would be good to get out of the city,' he went on. 'I thought I would hire a car.' He smiled at her. 'Perhaps you could suggest a suitable destination.'

She sat rather straighter. 'I really couldn't advise you.'

'No? You disappoint me.'

'I don't really know your tastes.' She hesitated. 'Do you like—looking at things?'

'I like to look at you.' The green eyes met hers with cool directness. 'As for the rest, I am not a sightseer, but I thought we might find a pleasant hotel in some beautiful part of England and spend the remainder of the weekend together there.'

He paused, running a hand over his chin. 'I need to shave, and we both have bags to pack. When I return you can tell me where you would like me to take you.'

She said quietly, 'After paradise, anywhere else will seem rather tame.'

There was an odd silence. Flora saw his mouth tighten, and the green eyes become suddenly remote. It was as if she had made him angry, she thought in bewilderment.

But when he spoke his voice was light. 'You flatter me, *carissima*. But you should beware of paradise. It can so often conceal a serpent.' He rose to his feet. 'I should not be longer than an hour or two.' He came round the table and dropped a kiss on her hair. 'Have our route planned.'

There was a nightgown in her drawer, a sheer, lacy thing wrapped in tissue, that she had bought for her honeymoon with Chris.

The betrayal was complete now, she thought, as she put it carefully into her weekend case. And the wretchedness of telling Chris would be her punishment.

She thought of phoning Hes. You're a witch, she'd say lightly. You wished it on me and it's happened. Passion to die for. *And then loneliness to last a lifetime.* Only she wouldn't say that.

Nor did she make the call. There would be plenty of time for confession in the weeks to come, she thought without joy.

But she did not have time to brood because, surprisingly, Marco was back within the hour, driving a low, sleek open-topped sports car.

Flora gaped at it. 'Someone let you hire that?' she asked incredulously.

'It belongs to Vittoria,' he said. 'She has lent it to me.' He paused. 'She also suggested somewhere we might go—unless, of course, you have thought of a place.'

She spread her hands. 'I've been racking my brains, but I so rarely go out of London—except to Surrey, to stay with my mother and stepfather.' And very occasionally to Essex and Chris's family, she thought with a pang of guilt.

'It is called the Aldleigh Manor Hotel,' he said. 'Vittoria says it is very comfortable, with beautiful grounds, and wonderful food.'

'It sounds perfect,' she said. 'Like a dream.'

His brows drew together. 'You would prefer somewhere else? That's not a problem. We could tour around, maybe? Take our chances?'

'Oh, no,' Flora said swiftly. 'Aldleigh Manor sounds really wonderful. But it might be fully booked.'

'They have a room for us,' he said quietly. 'Overlooking the lake. I must confess I already made the reservation. Although it can always be cancelled if you wish?'

'Certainly not.' Flora threw him a wicked grin. 'I can't wait to see it. And if it's anything short of paradise I shall know who to complain to.'

'You're very quiet,' she commented as they edged their way out of London.

'I am concentrating on my driving,' Marco returned after a pause. 'Remember that for me the gear shift— the road—everything is on the wrong side. And if I scratch Vittoria's darling—*Madonna!*—I'll be a dead man. And I have people depending on me back in Milan.'

'Are accountants really that important?' she teased.

'Only when they are as good as I am, *mia bella*.' He slanted a grin at her.

He really had no need to worry, she thought. He was a marvellous driver, considerate with other traffic, and not using the powerful car as an extension of his virility.

All she had to do was sit back and admire his profile, and bask in the envious glances of people toiling along hot pavements.

The hotel was important enough to be signposted.

'Oh,' Flora said. 'It has a golf course.'

'Well, that need not concern us,' Marco said, turning the car between tall stone gateposts. 'Unless you wish to hire clubs and play?'

'No, thanks,' she said hastily. It was just a reminder of Chris that she didn't need, she thought, guilt piling in again. Well, perhaps she could find some reason to tell Marco she didn't like the place, and persuade him to drive somewhere else.

But it was difficult to know what she could possibly object to, she thought, as the building itself came into view from the long curving drive. It was three storeys high, its grey stones lit by the late afternoon sun which gave the mullioned windows a diamond sparkle. The commanding entrance was made more welcoming by the urns of bright flowers which flanked it.

As Marco drew into one of the parking spaces allotted to hotel guests a porter instantly emerged to take their bags.

They were shown into a vast foyer, made cool by arrangements of tall green plants and dominated by a massive central staircase.

Through an open door Flora could see people sitting in a pretty lounge, enjoying afternoon tea.

She touched Marco's arm. 'That looks nice.'

He smiled at her. 'I'll have some sent up to our room. Wait for me here, *cara*, while I register.'

As he went to the desk Flora took off the scarf she'd been wearing and shook her hair free. She looked around her, noting where the lifts were and spotting discreet signs indicating the cocktail bar, the dining room and the leisure club. According to the brochure that she picked up from a side table, as well as an outdoor swimming pool the Manor boasted an indoor pool, together with a gymnasium and a sauna in its basement.

Perhaps I can interest Marco in some other form of exercise, she thought, suppressing a grin. Or, on second thoughts, perhaps not...

She heard her name spoken, and turned, the smile freezing on her lips as she did so.

Because it wasn't Marco with the key, as she'd expected.

It was Chris. Standing there in front of her with three other men, all carrying golf bags. Looking astonished, and not altogether pleased.

'Flora,' he repeated. 'What on earth are you doing here? How did you find me? Is something wrong?'

'No, nothing.' *Or everything*, she thought desperately. 'I didn't know you were here.' She gave a wild, bright smile. 'But I'm not actually staying. So, please, don't let me interfere with your game. Do go on, and I—I'll see you on Monday.'

'Oh, we've finished for the day,' Chris said. 'Not a bad couple of rounds at all. But you haven't met the lads. Jack—Barry—Neil, this is my fiancée, Flora Graham, who seems to be just passing through for some reason.' And he laughed with a kind of boisterous unease.

There was a chorus of greeting which faded into a bewildered silence, and Flora realised, horrified, that she'd actually taken a step backwards.

'So nice to see you all,' she babbled. 'But I really must be going.'

If I can just get outside and find the car I can wait in it. Tell Marco I can't stay…

She turned to flee, and cannoned straight into Marco himself. He steadied her, hands on her shoulders, halting her flight.

'You are going in the wrong direction, *carissima*.' He sounded amused, every word falling on her ears with total clarity. 'The lift is over there, and we are on the first floor—in the bridal suite, no less.' He slid his arm round her waist and pulled her close. His voice became lower, more intimate. 'I have asked them to send up your tea, and some champagne for us, so that we can—relax before dinner. Would you like that, my sweet one?'

The silence seemed to stretch out until doom. Except that doom would have been preferable, Flora thought. She felt as if she was watching everything from a distance—Chris looking stunned, with his mouth open and his face brick-red—his companions exchanging appalled glances and trying to edge away—and Marco, his hand resting on her hip in unquestioned possession, smiling like a fallen angel.

At last, 'Who are you?' Chris burst out hoarsely. 'And what the hell are you doing with my fiancée?'

Marco looked in his direction for the first time, his glance icy and contemptuous. And totally unwavering. He said, 'I am Marco Valante, *signore*, and I am Flora's lover. Is there anything more you wish to ask me?'

Flora saw Chris's mouth move, and realised he was silently repeating the name to himself. The angry colour had faded from his face and he was suddenly as white as a sheet.

There was tension in the air, harsh, almost tangible, filling the shaken silence.

'No,' Chris muttered at last. 'No, there's nothing.' And, without looking at Flora again, he turned and stumbled away, followed by his embarrassed companions.

'I think, *mia bella*,' Marco said softly, 'that your engagement is at an end.'

'You know the old cliché about praying for the floor to open and swallow you?' Flora threw a sodden tissue into the wastebin and pulled another from the box. 'Well, it's all true, Hes. I just wanted to disappear and never be found again.'

'Yet once again the floor remained intact,' said Hester. 'So what did you do? Go for the sympathy vote and throw up over Chris's shoes?'

'It's not funny.' Flora sent her a piteous look. 'Hes, it was the worst moment of my life, bar none.'

Twenty-four hours had passed, and they were in Flora's sitting room. Flora was stretched out on the sofa and Hester was standing by the window, glass of wine in hand.

She nodded. 'I believe you.' She whistled. 'Boy, when you fall off the wagon, Flo, you do it in spectacular style, I'll grant you that. No half-measures for our girl. So what happened next? I presume Chris tried to kill him?'

'No.' Flora shook her head drearily. 'He just stood there, looking at Marco as if he'd seen a ghost—or his worst nightmare. And then—he walked away.'

Hester frowned. 'You mean he didn't even take a swing at him? I'm not pro-violence, but under the circumstances...'

'Nothing,' Flora said tonelessly. 'And he didn't look at me, or say one word.'

Hester grimaced. 'Probably didn't trust himself.'

'I can hardly blame him for that,' Flora sighed. 'I can't forgive myself for the way I've treated him.'

'Let's talk some sense here.' Hester walked over, refilled her glass, then resumed her station at the window. 'I never felt that you and Chris were the couple of the year. You met and liked each other, and it—drifted from there.'

She shrugged. 'Maybe you'd both reached a stage where marriage seemed a good idea, and you were content to settle for just all right rather than terrific. It happens a lot, and in a lot of cases it probably works perfectly.

'But not for you, Flo. That red hair of yours gives you away. You're really an all or nothing girl, and sooner or later you'd have realised that. It's much better that it should happen now, before the wedding, even if the endgame was a bit drastic. But you didn't plan it that way, so stop beating yourself over the head. Ultimately it's all for the best.

'And, if it comes to that,' she added, frowning, 'why wasn't he here seducing you himself? If he hadn't been off with the lads, this Italian guy wouldn't have been able to get to first base with you.'

'We weren't joined at the wrist,' Flora objected.

'Or anywhere else, I gather,' Hester said drily.

She paused. 'Have you heard from Chris since it happened?'

'No,' Flora said bitterly. 'But I've had calls from practically all our families and friends. Clearly Chris recovered enough to get on the phone from the hotel and spread the bad word about me. By the time I got back here the answer-machine was practically bursting into flames. My mother—his mother—even my bloody step-sister banging on about little Harry's disappointment over the loss of his pageboy role.'

'Nightmare stuff,' said Hes. 'And universal condemnation, I suppose?'

Flora shrugged. 'My mother's disowned me completely. Says I've brought disgrace on the entire family and she'll never be able to hold her head up at the bridge club again. And, according to Chris's mother, in more right-thinking times I'd have been whipped at the cart's tail.'

'Prior to being stoned to death, I suppose,' Hester said acidly. 'Charming woman. Pity there isn't a public hangman any more. She'd have been ideal. Well, at least you've escaped having her as a mother-in-law. That's one bright spot amid the encircling gloom.'

She paused, then said carefully, 'And what about your Signor Valante? Has he been in touch since yesterday?'

'He drove me back here. I don't think either of us said a word. He brought in my bag and said he regretted the embarrassment he had caused me. And went.' Flora made a brave attempt at a smile. 'End of story.'

'Presumably because he's hideously embarrassed himself.' Hester sighed. 'After all, it was the most appalling coincidence to choose that hotel out of all the others you could have gone to.' She was silent for a moment. 'Whose decision was that, by the way?'

'It was Marco's suggestion, but he didn't pressure me into it. He said we could take pot luck somewhere else, if I wanted.' Flora shook her head. 'I should have obeyed my instincts and taken him at his word. Only Aldleigh Manor did sound lovely.'

'Wonderful,' Hester agreed drily. 'Just the place to meet one's friends.'

'Oh, don't.' Flora blew her nose, destroying another tissue. 'Anyway, it happened, and it's over. And Marco's gone. I just hope I never have to set eyes on him again,' she added, her voice cracking in the middle.

'Pity,' said Hester. 'I'd have liked to meet the man who finally made you into a woman. Because under all the woe, my lamb, there's a new light burning.' She gave her friend a worldly look. 'Nice, was it?'

'I don't want to discuss it.' Flora crunched another tissue in her hand.

'That good, eh?' Hester said reflectively. 'So what are your immediate plans, once you're over your crying jag?'

'I've got to get away for a while. I'd already been considering it, and now I'm sure. I feel bad enough about all this without having to field the angry phone calls,' she added, shuddering. 'I need to get myself back on track—somehow.'

'And you really don't want to see Marco Valante again?'

'Never—ever.'

'That's tough.' Hester came away from the window. 'Because he's outside, just getting out of a car.'

'Oh, God.' Flora scrubbed at her tearstained face. 'Don't let him in.'

'Nonsense.' Hester grinned at her as she went into the hall to answer the doorbell. 'I want to meet him, if you don't. I might even shake hands with him for his sterling efforts on behalf of repressed womanhood.'

'Hester!' Flora shrieked, but it was too late. The front door was being opened and there was a murmur of voices in the hall.

A moment later, Hester returned, her face wearing a faintly stunned expression. 'You have a visitor,' she said, standing aside to allow Marco to precede her into the room. 'And I have places to go and things to do, so I'm sure I leave you in good hands.'

'No—please. There's no need…' Flora began desperately, but Hester simply blew her a kiss, added an enigmatic wink, and departed.

Leaving Flora staring at Marco across the back of the sofa. She was horribly conscious of how she must look, in ancient jeans and a sweatshirt, her hair pulled back carelessly into a rubber band, her face pale without the camouflage of cosmetics, eyes reddened through weeping.

He, on the other hand, was immaculate, in another elegant suit, but his usual cool assurance was not as much in evidence. There was an odd tension about him, she realised. There were signs of strain in his face, the skin stretched tautly across the high cheekbones, and his eyes were watchful, even wary, as they studied her.

And yet, in spite of everything, she felt the familiar, shaming clench of excitement deep within her at the sight of him. The uncontrollable twist of yearning that she was unable to deny.

She felt more tears welling up suddenly—spilling over. He made a small, harsh sound in his throat and walked round the sofa to sit beside her. He took a spotless handkerchief from his pocket and began to dry her face, his touch gentle but impersonal.

When she was calm again he studied her gravely for a long moment. 'My poor little one,' he said quietly. 'Have you discovered you cared for him more than you knew?'

She shook her head. 'I wish I could say that,' she said

huskily. 'But it wouldn't be true. I—I would have broken off the engagement anyway, but I never meant it to happen like that. To publicly humiliate him in front of his friends.'

'Then why are you crying?'

Because, she cried out in her heart, I thought I would never see you again. Because I've just realised that, for me, it was never just sex. That, God help me, I've fallen in love with you. But I know you don't feel the same, so this has to be a secret I can never share—with anyone.

She gave a wavering smile. 'Perhaps because I've never had so many people concertedly angry with me before.' She swallowed. 'The general view is that I've done an unforgivable thing.'

He was silent for a moment. 'That is a harsh judgement,' he said at last. 'Engagements are broken every day.

'But not by me,' she said. 'I—I've always been so—well-behaved. And now I'm a bad lot. A scarlet woman, no less.'

He said her name, on a shaken breath, drawing her into his arms and holding her close. She flattened her hands against the breast of his shirt, absorbing the comforting warmth of his body, feeling the beat of his heart under her palm. Content, she realised, just to be near him. And how pathetic was that?

He took the band from her hair, running his fingers through the silky waves to free them, lingering over the contact. She could sense the pent-up longing in his touch, and her heart leapt.

'Your friend told me you are planning to go away for a while,' he said at last. 'Is that true?'

'Yes.' She bit her lip. 'I know I'm being a wimp, but

Chris seems to have told everyone about us, and I'd rather not face the music for a while.'

'Have you decided where to go?'

'Not yet.' She shook her head. 'I don't seem capable of active planning at the moment.'

'But your passport is in order?'

'Yes, of course.'

'Then that makes it simple,' he said. 'I shall take you back to Italy with me.'

Her lips parted in a soundless gasp. She stared up at him. 'You—can't be serious.'

'Why not?' He shrugged. 'I have to return there, and you need to escape. It solves several problems.'

And creates a hundred others. She thought it, but did not say it.

'Won't your family—your friends—find it—odd?'

'Why should they? I shall take you to the *castello*. I often have friends staying with me there.'

In translation, the *castello* was where he took his women, she told herself with a pang. She would be just another in a long line.

She ought to apply some belated common sense and return a polite but firm refusal, and she knew it. But he was leaving soon, and she wasn't sure that she could bear knowing this was the last time she would be in his arms, breathing the warm masculine scent of him, or feeling his lips touching hers.

She thought in agony, I can't let him go. I can't...

She said slowly, 'Marco—why do you want me with you?'

He put his lips to the agitated pulse in her throat. 'You have a short memory, *mia cara*.' The smile was back in his voice. That husky, sensuous note which sent her blood racing. 'Do you really not know?'

It was the answer she'd expected, so there was no point in regret or recrimination.

Heaven, she thought. Hell—and now heartbreak. Stark and inevitable, whether she stayed or went. But at least he would be hers—for a little while longer.

On a little whisper, she said, 'Do you think this is wise?'

'Ah, *mia bella*.' There was an odd note in his voice that was almost like sadness. 'I think it is too late for wisdom.'

'Yes,' she said, sighing. 'Perhaps so.' She tried to smile. 'In that case the answer's yes. I—I'll go with you, Marco.'

He took her hand and kissed it, then laid it against his cheek, his eyes closed, his face wrenched suddenly by some emotion that she did not understand.

But instinct told her it had nothing to do with happiness.

And she thought, Heaven help us both.

CHAPTER SIX

THEY flew to Italy three days later.

Flora had hardly had time to draw breath, let alone seriously question what she was doing.

She'd managed to reschedule the majority of her appointments. Only a few had taken umbrage and declared they would approach another company. So it seemed she would have a career to come back to when the bubble burst. As it surely would.

And, after an initial panic, Melanie had decided to enjoy being in charge for a short time, and was blooming under her new responsibilities.

One of the tasks Flora had considered essential had been to collect her engagement ring from the jeweller's and have it messengered over to Chris. So far he'd made no attempt to contact her, either at home or work, and she'd been thankful. But after that she'd expected an angry response, and had been surprised and relieved when there was only continuing silence.

Her mother, of course, had not been so reticent. Flora had called her reluctantly, to explain why she would not be available for the next couple of weeks, and had walked into another barrage of criticism and recrimination.

She was an embarrassment. She was ungrateful. She'd caused untold trouble and inconvenience over the wedding arrangements.

'And now you're actually going to Italy with this man.' Mrs Hunt's voice rose shrilly. 'Have you lost all sense of decency? My God, Flora, you know nothing about him. Why, he could be in the Mafia!'

Flora sighed. 'I don't think so, Mother,' she said with a touch of weariness. 'He's an accountant.'

'Well, that means nothing,' her mother said peevishly. 'They need people like him to—launder their money. I can't believe your behaviour, Flora,' she added. 'First you indulge in a sordid affair, and hurt your fiancé deeply. Now you could be mixing with criminals. You've disgraced us all, and I wash my hands of you.'

Flora bit her lip. 'Goodbye, Mother.' She spoke with resignation. 'I'll call you when I come back.'

'*If* you come back,' Mrs Hunt said ominously.

I'm glad I didn't mention Marco worked for a pharmaceutical outfit, Flora thought as she put the phone down, or she'd have said he was a drug dealer.

She decided to cheer herself with some retail therapy. However this stay in Italy turned out, it would be her first holiday in a considerable while. She had been too busy establishing her business to have time for overseas breaks.

For her honeymoon, of course, she'd have made an exception, she thought with a wintry smile.

But her wardrobe was seriously short of leisure gear, and she made a lightning raid on Kensington High Street to see what was available. There was some glamorous swimwear on offer, and she took her pick, choosing filmy sarongs and overshirts to go with her selection.

She packed with discrimination, reminding herself that she was packing for two weeks' holiday only—not a lifetime.

Now that the moment of departure was approaching, her nerves were bunching into knots.

She was stingingly aware that she'd hardly seen anything of Marco in the past forty-eight hours, although he had telephoned her several times. But he hadn't been round in person and there'd been no suggestion that he wished to spend the night with her.

And she missed him like hell.

All these years, she reflected wryly, she'd slept alone in her own bed, tranquil and untroubled.

Now, after those few brief hours in his arms, she was restless, forever reaching for him in the darkness and finding only an empty space beside her.

The words *Will I see you tonight?* had trembled on her lips more than once as they'd spoken on the phone, but she hadn't dared utter them.

Perhaps he was having serious second thoughts, she mused, wincing, and she would get a last-minute phone call making an excuse to withdraw his invitation.

If so, she decided proudly, she would be round to the nearest travel agent for a last-minute deal—anywhere but Italy.

She could not conceal her shock, however, when Marco arrived to collect her at the appointed time in a chauffeur driven car.

'You like to travel in style,' she commented, brows delicately lifted, as she watched the driver load her one modest case into the boot.

'So do you, *cara*.' Marco looked her over slowly, with an undisguised appreciation that played havoc with her pulses.

She was wearing a knee-length cream skirt, with a matching round-necked top in a silky fabric and a dark green linen jacket. She had her hair trimmed, and layered slightly too, so that it clung more smoothly to the shape of her head.

She might be trembling inside, but on the surface she looked confident—impeccable.

She tilted her chin, offering him a frankly sultry smile. 'I wonder what other surprises you have in store for me, *signore*.'

'Behave yourself, *mia bella*,' he warned softly. 'We have a plane to catch.'

And not just any old plane, Flora discovered. After being ushered with due deference into the VIP lounge at the airport, she found herself subsequently seated in the first-class area of the aircraft, with an attentive stewardess offering champagne.

She said shakily, 'Is this a company perk? They must think very highly of you.'

'I am revered,' Marco returned solemnly, but Flora had seen the flicker of amusement in his eyes and drew a deep breath.

'Marco,' she said, 'who actually owns Altimazza?'

He smiled ruefully. 'The Valante family, *cara*, and I am the chairman and principal shareholder.'

For a moment indignation held her mute, then she rallied. 'Then why have you been making a fool of me— letting me think you were just an employee—an accountant?'

'You didn't request to see my résumé, Flora *mia*.' He shrugged. 'And I *am* a qualified accountant. For the record, I have also studied law and business management,' he added. 'If you had asked, I would have told you.'

Wryly, he surveyed her flushed, mutinous face. 'Does it really make such a difference? We are both still the same people.'

'How can you say that?' Her voice shook a little. 'From the first you must have been laughing at me...'

'No,' he said quietly. 'That was never true—believe me.'

'Then what is the truth?' Flora asked stormily. 'That it amused you to play the prince in disguise, with me as some bloody Cinderella?'

His mouth tightened. 'I hardly found you in rags. But I admit that perhaps I had a foolish wish to be wanted for myself. It has not always been so in the past.'

'Oh, dear.' Her voice bit. 'You poor rich man. I bet you didn't turn down many of the offers, for all that.'

'What do you expect me to say?' Marco threw back at her. 'That I lived a celibate life while I was waiting for you? I will not insult you by such a pretence.'

It was her turn to shrug. 'What's one more among so many?'

'Why are you so angry?' he asked curiously.

'Because I feel stupid,' she said. 'And because I wonder what else you've been hiding.'

'One thing I never hid,' he said quietly. 'That I wanted you from the moment I saw you. And the only reason you are here at this moment is because we both wished it. And, for me, nothing has changed.'

He paused. 'However, I shall not force you to stay,' he added levelly. 'If it has become impossible for you to remain with me then I can arrange to have you flown anywhere else in the world you wish to go. The choice is yours, *carissima*.'

For a long moment she was silent, as her head and her heart fought a short, fierce battle.

Then she said in a stifled voice, 'There's nowhere else in the world I wish to go—and you know it.'

'Ah, *dolcezza mia*,' he said softly. 'Sometimes you tear me apart.'

She sat beside him, her hand clasped in his, and saw

the envy in the eyes of the pretty girls who waited on them. Who thought she'd won the jackpot—sexually, as well as in money terms.

And she smiled back, and thanked them for the lunch and hot towels, because they might be right. Because for the next two weeks she was going to be spoiled and cosseted by day, and taken to heaven each night.

And then it would be over. Midnight would strike and Cinders would be back in the real world.

But, for now, she was having a wonderful time—of course she was—with even better to come. And she had no illusions—no crazy naïve dreams about the possibility of a future with the man at her side. Or not any longer, anyway, she amended swiftly.

Her time with him was finite, and she accepted that.

So, there was no need for this niggling feeling of unease. No need at all.

And if I say it often enough, she thought, I may even begin to believe it.

But no uncertainty could cloud her first view of San Silvestro.

As the helicopter began its descent Flora saw the sun-baked stones of the *castello*, gleaming pink, grey and cream in the afternoon light as it reared up from the riot of greenery which surrounded it.

That first heart-stopping glimpse showed her a cluster of buildings, roofed in faded terracotta and surmounted by a square tower. Its clifftop setting had clearly been chosen with an arrogant eye for impact, and it lay, like a watchful lion, overlooking the azure sea.

For Flora, it was a fairytale image—a vision of Renaissance power—but for the man beside her, she realised, it was home. Emphasising the very different worlds they inhabited, she thought with sudden bleakness, picking out the turquoise shimmer of a swimming pool.

As the helicopter landed on a flat sweep of lawn at the rear of the *castello*, Flora could see people descending the steps from the imposing terrace and coming to meet them.

Her stomach clenched in swift nervousness.

The man leading the charge was tall, with silver hair. He was dressed in dark trousers and a discreet grey jacket, and the austerity of his features was relieved by a smile of sheer delight.

That must be Alfredo, Flora thought, remembering what Marco had been saying on the flight down.

'He is my *maggiordomo*, and Marta, his wife, is the housekeeper,' he'd told her. 'Alfredo's father worked for my grandfather, so he was born at the *castello*, like myself, and loves it as much.'

She found herself swallowing as Marco helped her alight from the helicopter, maintaining his firm grip on her hand.

'*Avanti,*' he said briskly, and they set off across the lawn towards the welcoming party, Flora struggling to match his long-legged stride.

After the warmth of his greeting for his master, Flora found Alfredo's calm correctness towards herself slightly daunting. She was also aware of the shrewdly assessing glances being directed at her by the rest of the staff as they were formally presented to her.

'This is Ninetta, *signorina*.' Alfredo indicated a plump, pretty girl in a dark dress and white apron. 'She will unpack for you, and attend you during your time with us.'

'*Grazie,*' Flora murmured, wryly reviewing the modest contents of her luggage.

Alfredo gave a stately inclination of the head. 'So, if you will follow me, *signorina*, I will show you to your room.'

As he went past Marco spoke to him softly and briefly in his own language. Just for a second the impassive mask slipped, and the major-domo let surprise show. But he recovered instantly, murmuring a respectful, '*Si, signore, naturalamente,*' as he set off for the house, snapping his fingers at Ninetta to pick up Flora's case.

Inside the *castello*, Flora received a whirlwind impression of large rooms with tiled floors, low ceilings and frescoed walls. Then she was ascending a wide stone staircase, walking along a gallery, navigating a long corridor and climbing another short flight of stone steps.

Alfredo opened the double doors at the top and bowed her into the room. Its square shape told her instantly that she was in the tower of the *castello*, and probably its oldest part, too.

She stared round her, her jaw dropping at the subdued magnificence of the tapestry-hung walls and vast canopied bed. There was little furniture, but the few pieces were clearly very old and valuable, and the ancient carpet spread on the gleaming wood floor was possibly priceless.

There were deep cushioned seats in the window embrasures, and on the wall opposite the bed long glass doors had been fitted into the stone, giving access to a balcony with a wrought-iron rail and a stunning view over the sea.

Alfredo, observing her reaction with discreet satisfaction, pointed to a door in the corner of the room. 'That is the *signore's* dressing room.' He opened another door in the opposite corner. 'And here—the bathroom, *signorina*.'

Peeping past him, Flora saw it contained a sunken bath as well as an imposing circular shower cubicle.

She said quietly, 'It's all—so beautiful. I can hardly believe I'm not dreaming.'

He bowed politely. 'Please tell Ninetta if there is anything you need, *signorina*.'

While the maid dealt speedily with the contents of her case Flora opened the balcony doors and went outside. Below her was a tangle of trees, the silvery shimmer of olives punctuated by the deep green of cypresses standing like tall sentinels, and she could see amongst them the paler line of a track going down towards the sea.

The air was warm, and heavy with the scent of flowers and the hum of insects. Slowly, Flora felt herself begin to relax.

When you're out of your depth—float, she told herself.

So when Marco came to stand behind her, and slid his arms round her waist, she leaned back in his embrace, smiling as his lips found the leaping pulse in her throat.

'Do you think you can like it here?' he whispered against her ear.

'It's really heaven on earth,' Flora returned softly. 'How can you bear to be away from it?'

'We all have work—other duties.' He paused. 'Sometimes they take us to places where we would rather not be.'

She pointed. 'Is that the path you used to take to the beach—you and Vittoria?'

'You remember that?' He sounded faintly surprised.

'Of course.' *I remember,* she thought, *every word you've ever said to me.* 'Will you show it to me?'

'Yes,' he said. 'I'll show you everywhere and everything. But later, *mia cara.*' His hands lifted, cupping her breasts. 'At the moment I have—other priorities.'

He drew her back into the shaded quiet of the room and she went unresistingly, raising her mouth to his.

As their lips met everything changed. Suddenly his kiss was a hunger—the fierce, driving need of a starving man. Gasping, Flora responded, her senses going wild under the onslaught.

They swayed together, as if caught in a storm wind. She felt his hands seeking her, running over her breasts, hips and thighs with a kind of desperation through the thin layer of clothing as his kiss deepened almost savagely.

At last he lifted his head, staring down into her flushed face, his eyes glittering like emeralds.

She heard herself say his name on a husky, aching sigh of pure longing.

Roughly Marco pushed the jacket from her shoulders, tugged at the zip of her skirt, dragging the loosened cloth down over her hips, lifting her free of it.

There was no sound in the room but the hoarse raggedness of their breathing and the rustle of clothing ruthlessly pulled apart and discarded.

Marco sank down to the floor, taking her with him. As he moved over her, her body opened for him in a demand as fierce as his own.

It was not a gentle mating. Their mutual desire was too wild—too urgent for that. Their hands and mouths clung, tore, ravaged, as their bodies fought their way to the waiting glory.

It was upon them almost before they knew it. Flora

cried out half in exhilaration, half in fear as she felt herself wrenched apart in a pleasure so dark and soaring that she thought she might die.

Almost fainting, she heard Marco crying out in an anguish of delight as he reached his own climax.

Afterwards she lay, supine, feeling the beloved weight of his head on her breasts, his arm across her body, his hand curved possessively round her hip. Lay very still, incapable of movement, speech or even thought.

Eventually it was Marco who stirred first. He raised himself and looked down at her, a sheen of moisture still clinging to his skin, his eyes remorseful.

'Did I hurt you?' he whispered. 'Tell me the truth, my sweet one, my heart.'

She smiled up at him, slowly, languorously, her lashes veiling her eyes. 'I don't remember,' she told him softly, her arms lifting to draw him down again. 'And I certainly don't care,' she added as her lips parted for his kiss.

After a while she said, 'Won't everyone be wondering where we are?'

'They are not paid to wonder,' Marco said lazily, his hand stroking her arm.

She gasped. 'Aren't you the autocrat? You just take all this for granted—don't you?'

'No, *mia bella*. I take nothing for granted. But I agree we cannot spend the rest of our lives here on the floor.' He got to his feet, pulling her up with him. 'We'll take a shower, then I'll show you the way down to the beach.'

'What about our clothes?' Flora looked with dismay at the crumpled garments strewn across the carpet.

'Leave them. They will be attended to.' Marco swept her briskly into the bathroom.

It seemed strange to share the shower with him. To

see her toiletries set out on the marble top beside his.
To know that her clothes were hanging beside his and
laid away in drawers in his dressing room.

She had never known this level of intimacy with anyone before, she realised blankly.

Even when she'd shared a flat with two other girls
she'd had her own room. Up to now she'd kept her space
inviolate—in more ways than one, she thought wryly,
remembering the pristine white bedroom in London.

And then Marco had invaded her life, overturning all
the careful structures and beliefs that she'd built up.
Taking her to another dimension. But only on a temporary basis, she reminded herself, pulling on a black
bikini and covering it with a black and white voile shirt.

And, she thought, thrusting sun oil and dark glasses
into her pale straw shoulder bag, she must never let herself forget that.

The grounds of the *castello* were a riot of blossom. As
they made their way down the path Flora was assailed
by scent and colour on all sides. Roses hung in a lovely
tangle over stone walls and the stumps of trees, studded
by the paler shades of camellias. Terracotta urns, heavy
with pelargoniums, marked each bend in the track,
which occasionally became shallow stone steps.

At one point their way was blocked by a tall wrought-
iron gate.

'My grandfather had it put there when I was a small
child,' Marco explained, releasing the catch. 'He wanted
to make sure I never went down to the beach to swim
unsupervised.'

'Oh,' she said. 'And did it work?'

'No.' He slanted a grin at her, and for a moment she

glimpsed the boy he'd once been. Her heart twisted inside her.

The cove was bigger than she'd expected. At one end there was a boathouse, and a small landing stage, at the other, separated by a crescent of pale sand, was a platform of flat rock.

'You can dive from that rock,' Marco said. 'The beach shelves quickly and very deeply. It is easy to get out of one's depth.'

She thought, I'm out of my depth now—and drowning.

Aloud, she said, 'Then I'll have to be careful.'

There were sun loungers on the sand, two of them, under a large striped umbrella. And under the shadow of the cliff was a small pavilion painted pale blue, with a pretty domed roof.

'It has changing rooms and a shower,' Marco explained, as if it was all a matter of course. 'Also a refrigerator with cold drinks.'

'Yes,' she said. 'Naturally it would have.'

His brows lifted. 'You disapprove?'

'No.' She pulled a face. 'I was just thinking of the poor souls who have to schlep down here to arrange the sun beds and refill the fridge.'

'They provide a service for which they are well paid,' he said, after a pause, adding drily, 'As you do yourself, *mia cara*.' He gave her a meditative look. 'Would you prefer me if I lived in a city flat without air-conditioning and cooked for myself?'

'No.' Her tone was defensive. She gestured wildly around her. 'I'm just not prepared for—all this.'

'I hoped San Silvestro would please you.'

'It does. It's unbelievably beautiful and I'm totally knocked out by it. But I'm Flora Graham, and I do live in the city, without air-conditioning, and I do my own cooking—and I don't know what I'm doing here.'

'You are here because I asked you, Flora *mia*. Because I wanted you to spend some time with me in a place that I love.' He stripped off the shirt he was wearing and held out his hand to her. 'Now, let us go for a swim.'

The water felt like warm satin against her skin. She swam, then floated for a while, looking up at the unsullied blue of the sky, then swam again, making her way over to the rocks. She clambered up on to one of them and perched there, wringing the water out of her hair.

After a few moments Marco joined her, bringing the sun oil with him.

'You must use this, *cara*, or you will burn.'

She applied the fragrant oil to her arms and legs, then handed him the bottle. 'Do my back for me, please?'

He dropped a kiss on her warm shoulder. 'The pleasure will be all mine,' he assured her softly. He undid the clip of her bikini top, pushing away the straps, and began to rub the oil into her skin with deft, light strokes. She moved luxuriously under his touch, lifting her face to the sun, smiling when his hands moved to her uncovered breasts.

Then felt him halt, tensing suddenly.

'Don't stop,' Flora whispered protestingly, teasingly.

'Listen.' His tone was imperative.

Mystified she obeyed, and heard the throb of an approaching engine. Next moment a boat, low, sleek and powerful, appeared round the headland, a solitary figure at its wheel.

Flora saw an arm lifted in greeting, then the boat turned into the cove, heading for the landing stage.

Marco said something quiet, grim, and probably obscene under his breath. Then, 'Cover yourself, *cara*,' he ordered.

Flora retrieved her bikini top and he clipped it swiftly into place.

By the time they had clambered down from the rocks the boat had come to rest and its occupant was on the landing stage, making it secure.

He was of medium height, and stockily built, with a coarsely handsome face. He was wearing minuscule shorts and a striped top, and he strutted towards them, his full mouth grinning broadly.

'*Ciao*, Marco. *Come va?*' He burst into a flood of Italian, his bold eyes raking Flora as he did so.

'Tonio,' Marco acknowledged coolly, his fingers closing round Flora's.

A gesture not lost on the newcomer. '*Ciao, bella. Come ti chiami?*'

Flora lifted her chin. 'I'm sorry, *signore*, but I don't speak your language.'

There was an odd silence. Then, '*Inglesa, eh?*' their visitor said musingly. 'Well, well.' The black eyes surveyed her unwinkingly. 'And what is your name, *bella ragazza?*'

'This is Flora Graham,' Marco intervened coldly. 'Flora, allow me to present Antonio Baressi.'

'But you must call me Tonio.' He gave her another lingering smile, then turned to Marco. 'What a wonderful surprise to find you here, my friend. I thought, after your successful mission, you would be keen to get back to your desk in Milan. Instead you are entertaining a charming guest. *Bravo.*'

Marco's mouth tightened. 'What are you doing here, Tonio?'

'Visiting Zia Paolina, naturally.' He allowed a pause,

then smote a fist theatrically against his forehead. 'But of course—you did not realise she was in residence. She will be fascinated to know that you are at the *castello*. May I take some message from you?'

On the surface he was all smiles, and eagerness to please, but Flora wasn't deceived. There was something simmering in the air, here, a tension that was almost tangible.

'Thank you,' Marco said with cool civility. 'But I shall make a point of contacting her myself.'

Tonio turned to Flora. 'My aunt is Marco's *madrina*— his godmother,' he explained. 'It is a special relationship, you understand. Since the sad death of his parents they have always been close.' The black eyes glittered jovially at her. 'But I am sure he has already told you this.'

Flora murmured something polite and noncommittal. The sun was blazingly hot, but she felt a faint chill, as if cold fingers had been laid along her spine, and found herself moving almost unconsciously slightly closer to Marco.

'You must bring Signorina Flora to meet Zia Paolina,' Tonio went on. 'She will be enchanted—and Ottavia, too, *naturalamente*.' He dropped the name like a stone into a pool, then gave them an insinuating glance. 'Unless, of course, you would prefer to be alone.'

'*Si*,' Marco said softly, his hand tightening round Flora's. 'I think so.'

Tonio shrugged. 'How well I understand. In your shoes I would do the same.' He kissed the tips of his fingers, accompanying the gesture with a slight leer. 'You are a fortunate man, *compagno*, so why waste valuable time paying visits?'

Marco said, very softly, 'Or receiving them...'

'Ah.' The other's smile widened. 'A hint to be gone. You wish to enjoy each other's company undisturbed. *Si, capisce. Arrivederci, signorina.* I hope we meet again.'

That, thought Flora, is the last thing I want. But she forced a smile. 'Thank you.'

As they stood, watching the boat heading out to sea again, she stole a glance at Marco, aware of him rigid beside her, his face expressionless.

She said, quietly and clearly, 'What a squalid little man.'

There was a silence, then she felt him relax slightly. He turned to her, his smile rueful.

'Indeed,' he said. 'And today he was relatively well-behaved.'

She hesitated. 'We don't—have to see him again, do we?'

'I hope not.' Marco's mouth tightened. 'But, as you see, he does not always wait for an invitation.'

She said slowly, 'He'd need a hide like a rhinoceros to come back. You were hardly welcoming.'

'I have my reasons.'

She bit her lip. 'Are you going to tell me what they are?'

'Perhaps one day,' he said, after a silence. 'But not now. Not yet.' He moved his shoulders briefly, almost irritably, as if shaking off some burden. 'Do you wish to swim again, *cara*, or shall we go back to the house? Has that fool spoiled the afternoon for you?'

'He's spoiled nothing. And he's gone. So I'd like to stay for a while—catch the last of the sun.' Flora moved over to one of the sun loungers and lay down on it. As Marco stretched himself silently beside her she looked at him, aware of his air of preoccupation.

She said suddenly, 'Marco, if you feel you should visit your godmother, then that's fine with me. I'll be perfectly happy to stay here.'

'Do not concern yourself, *carissima*. I have more than fulfilled my obligations to her, believe me.'

He spoke quietly, but she could hear an underlying note of almost savage anger in his voice, and was shaken by it.

There were undercurrents here, she thought, staring sightlessly at the sky, that she could not begin to understand. But, then, her comprehension wasn't required, she reminded herself with a pang. His other relationships were none of her business. Because she was here to share Marco's bed, not his problems.

So she wouldn't ask any more questions about Zia Paolina.

Nor would she permit herself to speculate about the unknown Ottavia, and her place in the scheme of things. After all, Marco had enjoyed a life before he met her, and that life would continue after she was gone. She couldn't allow that to matter.

But then she remembered the satisfaction in Tonio's voice when he'd pronounced the name—the gloating relish in his black eyes—and she knew that Ottavia could not be so easily dismissed.

She thought suddenly, Tonio's the serpent that Marco warned me about—the serpent waiting for me here in paradise.

And found herself shivering, as if a dark cloud had covered the sun.

CHAPTER SEVEN

IT WASN'T really a cloud, Flora decided. It was more a faint shadow. Yet she was aware of it all the time.

It was there in the sunlit days, while she and Marco went to the beach, swam in the pool, played tennis, and explored the surrounding countryside.

While they dined by candlelight, or sat on the moonlit terrace, drinking wine and talking, or listening to music.

It was even there at nights, when he made love to her with such exquisite skill and passion, or soothed her to sleep in his arms.

And the time was long past when she could have said totally casually, Who is Ottavia?

To ask now would be to reveal that it was preying on her mind. That it had come to matter. And she couldn't let him know that.

Because she had no right to concern herself. The parameters of their relationship were in place, and there was no space for jealousy.

There had been no more unwelcome visitors. In fact, no visitors at all. The real world was hardly allowed to intrude.

Flora was wryly aware how quickly she'd adapted to life at the *castello*, where unseen hands seemed to anticipate her every wish.

It was the quiet, impassive presence of Alfredo, she knew, that made San Silvestro run with such smooth efficiency. And, whatever his private views on her presence, he treated her invariably with soft-voiced respect.

Which was more than could always be said for Ninetta, Flora acknowledged frowningly. And it was just unfortunate that she had more to do with her than any of the other servants at the *castello*.

Not that the girl was overtly insolent, or lazy. There was just something—sometimes—in her manner which spoke of a buried resentment. The occasional suggestion of a flounce, and a faint curl of the full lips when Flora requested some service.

Not that it happened often. However much Marco might tease her about it, Flora could no more leave her clothes lying around for someone else to pick up, or abandon wet towels on the bathroom floor than she could fly. But sometimes she felt that Ninetta might have thought better of her if she'd done exactly that.

Or perhaps the girl was just tired of having to run round after yet another of the *signore's* mistresses, she thought, with a stifled sigh. Although she could never ask her that, of course. Or whether Ottavia had ever been one of them…

She firmly closed off that line of questioning. She had to learn to live entirely for the present, she told herself. It was pointless concerning herself about the past, or even worrying over the future, because both were out of her hands.

So, it would be one day at a time, and no more, and what was the problem with that when she was so happy?

And no one, she thought, could ever take that away from her.

The boathouse, Flora had soon learned, was not just for show. It contained a speedboat, which Marco used mainly for water-skiing, as well as his windsurfer, and a sailing boat—the *Beatrice II*.

'My father built the first one, and named it for my mother,' he told Flora when he took her sailing the first time, standing behind her, steadying her hands on the wheel. 'I decided to continue the tradition.'

'Did she like to sail?' Flora found she was revelling in this swoop along the coast, her ear already attuned to the slap of water against the bow and the song of the wind in the sails above her.

He shrugged. 'My father loved to—and she loved to be with him. She even watched him play polo, which terrified her. And she was his first passenger when he got his pilot's licence.' There was a taut silence. 'And, of course, his last.'

Flora was very still. Marco knew every detail of her family background, but up to now had said very little about his own. Perhaps this new candour would drive away the faint mist which seemed to hang between them.

'There was an accident?' Tentatively, she broke the brooding quiet.

'Some kind of mechanical failure.' His tone was brusque with remembered pain. 'They were flying down here from Rome for my grandfather's birthday. I had been allowed home from school for the occasion too, and I remember going with Nonno Giovanni to meet them at the airfield, whining because they were so late and I was getting bored.

'And then someone came and called my grandfather away into another room. I could watch him through the glass partition, although I could not hear what was being said. But I saw his face—and I knew.'

'How—how old were you?' Flora asked, her heart twisting.

'I was ten. Usually I flew with them too, and I had been angry because they had gone to Rome without me, to collect Nonno Giovanni's birthday gift.'

He shook his head. 'To this day I do not know what it was they had bought for him. But it could never have been worth the price they paid for it.'

She said quietly, 'Marco—I'm so sorry. I—I had no idea, even though you've always talked about your grandfather rather than your parents. It must have been terrible for you.'

'Yes,' he agreed. 'It was a bad time for us all. And I hardly had time to mourn before Nonno Giovanni began to train me as the next head of the family and the future chairman of Altimazza.'

She gasped. 'But you were just a small child.'

'The circumstances demanded that I grow up quickly,' Marco said drily. 'That I should understand and accept the responsibilities waiting for me.'

She leaned back against him. Her voice was husky. 'And when you became a man, what if you'd decided that kind of life wasn't for you?'

'Ah, *mia cara*, that was never an option.' He was silent for a moment. 'Only once was I offered a choice— and then I chose wrongly.' His voice was suddenly harsh.

She said hesitantly, 'But now you're free—surely?'

His arms tightened around her. She felt his mouth, gentle on the nape of her neck. 'I want to believe that, *mia bella. Dio*—how much I want to believe it.' There was a note almost of anguish in his tone.

He said no more, and she did not like to probe further.

Later they anchored in a small bay and swam, then picnicked on board. Afterwards, Marco made love to her with slow, passionate intensity, his eyes fixed almost painfully on her face, as if asking a question he dared not speak aloud.

What is it, my love? her heart cried out to him. *Ask me—please...*

When they arrived back at San Silvestro Alfredo was waiting on the landing stage, grave-faced.

'There has been a telephone call, *signore*—from the laboratories. They need to speak urgently with you.'

Marco cursed softly, then turned to Flora. 'Forgive me, *carissima*. I had better see what they want.' He set off up the path to the house, with Alfredo behind him, leaving Flora to follow more slowly.

She had showered and put on a slip of a dress, sleeveless and scoop-necked in an ivory silky fabric which showed off her growing tan, by the time Marco came into the room, his face serious and preoccupied.

He said without preamble, 'Flora, I have to go to Milan straight away. We have been conducting tests on a new drug to help asthma sufferers, which we believe could be a real breakthrough, but there seem to be problems—something which I must deal with immediately.'

'Oh.' Flora put down her mascara wand. 'Do you want me to come with you?'

'I think you would be too much of a distraction, *mia bella*.' His tone was rueful. 'Stay here and relax, and I will be back in a couple of days.'

'Then shall I pack for you?'

He shook his head. 'Alfredo has already done so. The helicopter is coming for me very soon.'

He came across to her and pulled her to her feet. 'I hate to leave you, *carissima*.' His tone thickened. 'But this is important.'

'Of course. And I'll be fine.' She smiled up at him, resolutely ignoring the ball of ice beginning to form in the pit of her stomach. Because this enforced absence would eat into the diminishing amount of time she had to spend with him. 'Alfredo will look after me.'

'You have won his heart.' He raised her hand to his lips. 'And that of everyone here.'

Apart from Ninetta. She thought it, but did not say it. Then Marco was kissing her, and she stopped thinking, offering herself totally the yearning demand of his mouth. Aware of nothing but the warmth and strength of him against her.

At last he almost tore his lips from hers. 'I must go,' he muttered huskily. 'I have to change my clothes.'

Left alone, Flora could hear the steady beat of the helicopter's approach. Coming, she thought, with a stab of anguish, to take him away. And it was ridiculous to feel so bereft—so scared—when he would be back so soon.

It must be the story about his parents which was weighing so heavily on her, she thought with a shiver.

When he emerged from his dressing room he looked almost alien in the formal dark suit. Flora looked across the room and saw a stranger.

Her smile was so forced it hurt. 'Please—take care.' *Or take me with you.*

'My heart's sweetness.' He looked back at her with passionate understanding. He took half a step towards her, then deliberately checked. 'I shall come back. And then I must talk to you.' He paused. 'Because there are things to be said. Issues, alas, that can no longer be avoided.'

He's going to tell me it's over, Flora thought, with a lurch of the heart. *That all good things must end. That it's time we returned to our separate worlds and got on with our lives.*

With a courage she had not known she possessed, she lifted her chin, went on smiling. 'I'll be here,' she said. 'Waiting.'

She went out on to the balcony and watched the helicopter take off and whirl away over the trees. Stood, a hand shading her eyes, until it vanished, and the throb of the engine could be heard no longer.

Her hands tightened on the balustrade as she fought the tears, harsh and bitter in her throat.

Only a couple of days, she reminded herself as she turned and trailed desolately back into the room. She could surely survive that.

But her real dread was the nights that she would spend alone in that enormous bed, without his arms around her in the darkness, or his voice drowsily murmuring her name as they woke to sunlight dappling through the window shutters.

And all those other endless nights to come, when she returned to England...

She pressed a clenched fist fiercely against her trembling mouth.

She'd known the score from the first, yet she'd allowed herself to be seduced by the atmosphere at the *castello*. To drift into a dream world where she and Marco stayed together always. Which was crazy.

It felt so right for her, she thought, but that did not guarantee that he necessarily shared her view. He was looking for entertainment, not commitment. Besides, he was a wealthy man. When the time came he would be sharing his life with a girl from his own social milieu.

As for herself—well, she was back in the real world now, and she was not going to allow herself to fall to pieces.

And if there was heartbreak ahead, maybe it was no more than she deserved for what she'd done to Chris.

She'd betrayed him totally, and yet, she realised guiltily, this was the first time she'd even spared him a thought. He seemed to belong to some distant, unreal part of her life. But he was flesh and blood, would be hurting because of her, and he deserved to have his pain acknowledged.

I was unfair to him from the start, she thought sadly. And particularly when I said I'd marry him. But we'd been seeing each other regularly for months and it seemed the next, logical progression. And—somehow— I persuaded myself that I loved him enough for marriage.

Because I didn't know what love could be—not then.

I should have known it couldn't work—after that one disastrous night. I should have stopped it there and then.

She'd been trying for weeks to parry Chris's growing insistence on making love to her. Finally she'd simply run out of excuses.

She couldn't even explain her own reluctance. After all, she wasn't a child, and it had been a natural stage in her relationship with the man she planned to marry. A man, moreover, who was good-looking, undeniably virile, and eager for her.

Yet the fact that she'd still been able to resist the increasing ardour of Chris's kisses should have been warning enough that all was not well.

She'd felt paralysed with awkwardness from the moment she'd arrived at Chris's flat and found the scene set with candles, flowers and music playing softly. There had even been a bottle of champagne chilling on ice.

Like something from Chapter Two of *The Seducer's Handbook*, she'd thought, wanting at first to laugh, and then, very badly, to run away.

And that had been the only real desire she'd experienced. She'd felt only numb as Chris had undressed her almost gloatingly. He hadn't been selfish. She knew that now. He had done his best to arouse her, holding his own excitement and need in check.

And she'd held him, eyes closed, and whispered, 'Yes,' when he'd asked if she was all right.

But it hadn't been true. Because everything about it had been wrong. And the pain of his first attempt to enter her had made her cry out as her muscles locked in shocked rejection.

She'd pushed him away almost violently, her frozen body slicked with sweat. 'No—I can't—please...'

He'd been kind at first, understanding. Had even comforted her. But it had soon become evident that he was determined to try again.

And each time her mind had gone into recoil as her body closed against him.

And eventually he'd become impatient, then really angry, and finally sullenly accepting.

'You have a real problem, Flora,' he'd flung at her over his shoulder as he reached for his clothes. 'I suggest you get yourself sorted, and soon. Maybe you should see a doctor—or a therapist.'

And she'd buried her shamed, unhappy face in the pillow and thought that perhaps he was right.

Until Marco had looked at her—touched her hand—kissed her. Made her burn for him. Established his possession of her long before the physical joining of their bodies. Transformed her surrender into glory.

When Chris had come back from his holiday in the Bahamas, she'd expected him to exert increasing pressure on her to go to bed with him, and had steeled herself to agree, telling herself it could never be that bad again.

But their time apart seemed to have engendered a more philosophical attitude in him, and he'd made no more attempts to force the issue.

Perhaps he'd thought that patience would eventually bring him his reward. Or maybe he'd simply been waiting for her to tell him that the medical treatment she hadn't even sought had been successful.

She had been telling herself that once they were married and settled they would have all the time in the world to work out their sexual relationship. That compatibility was not necessarily instant.

That Chris would make a good husband—the best— and sex was not the whole of a marriage.

Every excuse under the sun.

And I—almost—made myself believe them, she thought. I could have gone through with it. Only Hes wasn't fooled for a minute. And, of course, Marco, who looked into my eyes and saw that I was completely un-awakened.

Well, no one would think that now, she told herself with a wry smile at the mirror as she walked to the door, on her way downstairs to her first solitary dinner.

As she'd feared, time hung heavy on her hands without him.

He telephoned, of course. Hurried calls during the day between meetings that were not going well. And longer, more personal conversations late into the evening, which sent her to bed burning and restless.

He does it deliberately, she thought, twining her arms round his pillow and pulling it close. He would have to be punished on his return, and she knew exactly how. And she drifted off to sleep at last, smiling like a cat.

He'd been gone for three days when he finally called to say he would be home the following evening.

At last, her heart sang, but aloud she said sedately, 'Has the problem with the tests been sorted?'

He sighed. 'Alas, no. There is a serious flaw in the product, as I have suspected for some time, and we may have to start again from the beginning. I am authorising a new research programme, with a new director,' he added with a touch of grimness. 'Dr Farese believed he could take advantage of my absence and push the new drug through by cutting down the testing process. He knows differently now.'

Flora was silent for a moment. Then she said with slight constraint, 'Has all this happened because you've been spending too much time with me?'

'A little, perhaps.' His tone was rueful. 'But I do not regret one moment of it, Flora *mia*. However, it means that I must devote more time to Altimazza from now on.'

Her hand tightened round the receiver. 'Yes—yes, of course.'

'But enough of that.' He paused. 'Have you missed me?'

She knew that now, of all times, she ought to play it cool—make some flip, teasing remark. Instead she heard herself say yearningly, 'Oh, so much.' She took a deep breath. 'I'm going to tell Marta to have everything you most like for dinner—pasta with truffles, and that veal thing. Unless you'd prefer the chicken…?'

He was laughing. 'Choose what you will, *bellissima mia*. I am hungry only for you.'

She said with sudden shyness, 'And I for you, Marco.'

'Then imagine that I am with you, *cara*.' His voice sank huskily, intimately. 'That I am holding you naked—touching you as you like to be touched. You remember, hmm?'

'Marco!' She felt the fierce charge of desire deep within her. The swift scalding heat between her thighs. Her voice pleaded with him unsteadily. 'You're not being fair.'

'No,' he conceded softly. 'Perhaps not. But when I come back, my sweet one, there will be complete honesty between us—whatever the cost.'

She could hear the note of sadness in his voice and flinched from it, knowing what it must mean. He was warning her that their brief, rapturous idyll was drawing to an end.

She took a deep breath. She said quietly, 'I—I can't wait to see you.'

'It will not be long now,' he told her. 'But I must go. They are waiting for me.'

She returned his murmured, *'Arriverderci,'* and put down the telephone, standing for a moment, staring into space, realising she was going to need every scrap of emotional courage she possessed to get her through the next few days.

She heard a brief sound, and turned to see Ninetta standing in the doorway, watching her. She gasped. 'Oh—you startled me.'

'Scusi, signorina.'

The apology was meek enough, but Flora was certain that she'd detected a smirk in the dark eyes before they were deferentially lowered.

She said coolly, 'Did you want something, Ninetta?'

'I came to see if you needed me, *signorina.*' The girl came further into the room. 'You look pale. Have you had bad news?'

'On the contrary.' Flora met the sly glance head-on,

her chin lifted. 'The *signore* is coming back tomorrow. I am going to arrange a special dinner for him and I have to decide what to wear.'

Which wouldn't be easy, she acknowledged with an inward sigh. Travelling light had its disadvantages, and Marco had already seen everything she'd brought with her.

'Maybe it is an occasion for a new dress, *signorina*. Rocello has some good shops.'

It was about the first helpful remark Ninetta had ever made, and Flora sent her a surprised glance.

'Yes,' she agreed slowly. 'Perhaps it is.'

She might as well go out in style, she thought, with all flags flying. And she could use the time, as well, to buy some going-home presents—although apart from Hester and Melanie she couldn't think of many people who would welcome one from her.

She paused. 'Is there a morning bus into the town?'

For a moment Ninetta looked genuinely shocked. 'A car and driver will be provided for you, *signorina*. I shall arrange it at once. The *signore* would wish it,' she added, pre-empting any further objections that Flora might have.

I only wish, Flora thought when she was alone again, that I liked her better.

'I understand that you wish to go into town,' Alfredo said as he served her breakfast next morning. 'If you had consulted me, *signorina*, I would have escorted you myself. As it is, young Roberto will be driving you.'

'I'm sure he'll be fine.' Flora placated him, aware that his normally smooth feathers were ruffled. 'You must have far better things to do than wait while I shop.'

'Nothing I could not have postponed.' He was frowning slightly. 'The *signore* placed you in my charge, after all.'

'Well, Roberto will be a perfectly adequate stand-in.' She smiled at him. 'And I'll only be gone an hour or so.' She paused. 'Have I come across Roberto before?'

'I think not, *signorina*. He usually works in the grounds, but he drives the cars on occasion. He is the brother of Ninetta, who waits on you.'

Then I only hope he's more civil, Flora thought as she finished her meal.

Roberto seemed to be a rather stolid young man, with a limited command of English, so the journey into town was completed mostly in silence. However, the views from the winding coast road were sufficiently spectacular to compensate for any lack of conversation.

Rocello was not a large town, but its central square, overlooked by a fine Gothic church, was an imposing one.

Flora arranged to meet the taciturn Roberto by the church in two hours, which would give her time to make her purchases and, hopefully, do a little sightseeing too.

Ninetta had been right about the shops, she soon discovered. There were some delectable boutiques hidden away among the winding side streets, and she soon found a dress she liked—one of her favourite slip styles, with narrow straps and a fluid drift of a skirt, in white, with a stylised flower in crystal beads on the bodice.

A few doors away she came upon a local silversmith, and bought a pair of pretty earrings for Mel, and an elegant chain with twisted links for Hes.

In a small gallery near the square there was a small framed painting of the *castello*, and, after some heart-searching, she decided to buy it. In the days ahead it might help convince her that this had not been all a fantastic dream, she thought wryly.

It was going to be a very hot day, and Flora was quite glad to seek shelter in the shadowy interior of the church, which was famous for its frescoes painted, it was said, by a pupil of Giotto.

But, even so, she still had some time to while away before her appointment with Roberto. She stationed herself under the striped awning of one of the pavement cafés opposite the church, so that she could spot him as soon as he arrived.

She ordered a *cappuccino* and sat nibbling some of the little almond biscuits that came with it, idly watching the tourists, who were milling around with their cameras.

'Signorina Graham. I thought there could not be two women with that glorious shade of hair.'

Flora looked up in surprise to find Tonio Baressi smiling down at her.

'Oh,' she said slowly. 'Good morning.'

He drew out the chair opposite with a flourish. 'May I join you?'

'You seem to have done so already, *signore*.' Flora stole a surreptitious glance at her watch, hoping that Roberto might be early.

If Tonio noticed the tart note in her voice he gave no sign, merely signalling imperiously to the waiter.

'So Marco has gone to Milan and left you to your own devices,' he said, when his espresso arrived. He clicked his tongue. 'But how unchivalrous.'

'He has work to do,' Flora said shortly. My first time in Rocello, she thought, and I have to run into him.

He laughed. 'Whereas you are strictly for his leisure moments, eh? He is very fortunate to have found a woman so understanding of his—other obligations.'

Flora made a business of collecting together her packages. 'You must excuse me,' she said brightly. 'I'd like to have a look inside the church before my driver comes.'

'But surely I saw you coming out of the church a short while ago? You must find those frescoes particularly fascinating.' He was still smiling, but his eyes had narrowed. 'Or did Marco warn you to shun my company?'

'Of course not. How ridiculous.' She bit her lip in vexation, and a certain unease. How long had he been watching her, she wondered, and why?

'I am relieved to hear it. Please—have another *cappuccino*. I insist.'

She thanked him with a forced smile and sat back, trying to look relaxed, while scanning the passing crowd for Roberto.

'I hope you have enjoyed your stay at San Silvestro,' Tonio went on after a pause. 'It is unfortunate that all good things must end, no?'

She gave him a composed look. 'Actually, I still have some holiday left.'

'Yes, but it is hardly the same for you now that Marco has remembered his responsibilities to Altimazza. He can hardly be expected to commute to Milan on a daily basis. And the *castello* can be a lonely place.'

Her smile was taut. 'Please don't concern yourself about me, Signor Baressi. It really isn't necessary.'

'Call me Tonio, I beg. I assure you that I only wish to be your friend.'

'Thank you.' She reached for her bag and extracted enough money to pay for her own coffee. 'That's kind of you, but now I must be going.'

He said, almost idly, 'If you are expecting Roberto,

he has gone back to San Silvestro. I told him I would bring you back to the *castello* myself.'

Flora's lips parted in a gasp of sheer outrage. 'Then you had no right to do any such thing,' she exclaimed heatedly. 'And I prefer to make my own way back. I'll find a taxi…'

His grin was unrepentant. 'You fear I shall make advances to you?' He shook his head. 'I shall not. I offer friendship only. Something you may welcome before long,' he added softly. 'So let us have no more nonsense about taxis. It will be my pleasure to drive you.'

Flora lifted her chin. She said crisply, 'In that case I'd like to leave straight away. Roberto is going to find himself in real trouble with Alfredo for deserting me like this. He could even be sacked.'

He shrugged. 'He will easily find another job.'

Tonio also drove a sports car, but a considerably flashier example than the one Marco had used in London. He also considered himself a far better driver than he actually was, and Flora found herself cringing more than once.

When the coast road was suddenly abandoned, and they turned inland, she stiffened. 'This isn't the way to San Silvestro.'

'A small detour.' He was totally at ease. 'To the other side of the headland. My aunt, the Contessa Baressi, has expressed a wish to meet you. I know you would not wish to disappoint her.'

She said curtly, 'I would have preferred to be consulted in advance. And if Marco wishes me to know his godmother, then he's quite capable of arranging it.'

'Marco,' he said, 'is in Milan.'

'Yes, but he'll be back this evening. I can mention her invitation then…'

'My aunt wishes to see you now,' he said softly. 'And her requests are invariably granted. Even by Marco.' He paused. 'The two families have always been very close. And he and the Contessa have a very special relationship.'

'All the more reason,' she said, 'for him to be there.'

'Unfortunately, the Contessa intends to return to Rome very shortly. She was anxious to make time for you before her departure.'

He turned the car through a stone gateway, following a wide curving driveway up to the house.

It was a large, formal structure, built of local stone over three storeys.

The grounds were neat and well-kept, and an ornate fountain played before the main entrance, but for Flora it lacked the wilder appeal of the *castello*. Or was that simply because she was there under a kind of duress?

She sat very straight in her seat as Tonio brought the car to a halt.

'Please,' she said. 'Will you make some excuse to your aunt and take me back to San Silvestro?'

'Impossible, *mia cara*. She does not take disappointment well.'

He came round and opened her door. His hand gripped her arm, his smile openly triumphant as he observed her pallor—her startled eyes.

He said softly, '*Avanti*. Let's go.'

And he took her up the steps and into the house.

CHAPTER EIGHT

ENTERING the house was like walking into a cave. The hallway was vast and lofty, but also very dark. Flora was acutely conscious of Tonio's hand on her arm, urging her forward. As the elderly maid who had greeted them reached a large pair of double doors and flung them open she shrugged herself free of his grasp with unconcealed contempt, then walked forward, her head held high.

She found herself in a large room, with tall windows on two sides. Although she could at least see where she was going, the heavy drapes and the plethora of fussy furniture made her surroundings seem no less oppressive.

While the atmosphere of hostility, she thought, drawing a swift startled breath, resembled walking into a force field.

And it had to be generated by the two people who were waiting for them.

The Contessa Baressi was a tall woman, with steel-grey hair drawn into an elaborate chignon and the traces of a classic beauty in her thin face. The hands that gripped the arms of her brocaded armchair blazed with rings, and there was a diamond sunburst brooch pinned to the shoulder of her elegant black dress.

The other occupant of the room was standing by one of the windows, staring out. She was much younger— probably in her early twenties, Flora judged. She had a voluptuous figure, set off by her elegant pink linen sun dress, and a mane of black hair cascaded over her shoulders, framing a face that would have been pretty in a kittenish way except for its expression of blank misery. Her entire body was rigid, except for her hands, which were tearing monotonously at the chiffon scarf she was holding. She did not turn to look at the new arrivals, nor give any sign that she was aware of their presence.

Intuition told Flora that this must be the Ottavia on whom she'd expended so many anxious moments, and that her unease might well have been justified.

'Zia Paolina.' Tonio walked to his aunt and kissed her hand with easy deference. 'Allow me to present to you Marco's latest little friend, the Signorina Flora Graham.'

The Contessa's carefully painted mouth was fixed in a thin smile, but the eyes that looked Flora up and down were lizard-cold.

She said in heavily accented English, 'I am glad you could accept my invitation, *signorina. Grazie.*'

'You speak as if I had a choice,' Flora returned, meeting the older woman's gaze defiantly. 'Perhaps you would explain why you've had me brought here like this.'

'You do not think I wish to be acquainted with my *figlioccio's*—companions?'

'Frankly, no,' Flora said steadily. 'I'd have thought myself beneath your notice.'

She heard a sound from the direction of the window like the hissing of a small snake.

The Contessa inclined her head slightly. 'Under normal circumstances you would be right. But you, *signorina*, are quite out of the ordinary. And in so many ways. Which made our meeting quite inevitable, believe me.'

'Then I must be singularly dense,' Flora said. 'Because I still can't imagine what I'm doing here.'

The thin brows rose. 'Not dense, perhaps, but certainly a little stupid, as a woman in thrall to a man so often is. My godson's charm has clearly bewitched you—even to the point where you were prepared to break off your engagement and follow him to another country.' She gave a small metallic laugh. 'Such devotion, and all of it, alas, wasted.'

Flora's heart missed a beat. The Contessa, she thought, seemed to know a lot about recent events, even though her view of them was slanted.

She said, 'I think that's our business—Marco's and mine.'

'Ah, no,' the older woman said softly. 'It was never that exclusive, believe me.' She paused. 'Did you know that Marco had also been engaged to be married?'

'Yes.' It dawned on Flora that she knew where this conversation was leading. 'But I understood that had been broken off too.'

'Tragically, yes,' the Contessa acknowledged. 'It was a perfect match, planned from the time when they were both children.'

Flora glanced at the still figure by the window, with the busy, destructive hands. She said softly, 'Only his *fidanzata* preferred another man.'

The Contessa reared up like a cobra preparing to strike. 'Like you, poor child, she was seduced—betrayed by passion. And because of this she ruined her life. Threw away her chance of true happiness.'

'I'm sorry.' Flora stood her ground. 'But I don't see how this concerns me. I'd really like to go home now.'

'Home?' The plucked brows rose austerely. 'Is that how you regard the *castello*? You are presumptuous, *signorina*.'

Flora bit her lip. 'It was just a figure of speech.'

There was a silence, then the Contessa said, 'Be so good as to tell us how you met my godson.'

'We happened to have lunch in the same restaurant,' Flora admitted reluctantly. 'As I was leaving someone tried to snatch my bag, and Marco—came to my rescue.'

'Ah,' said the Contessa. 'Then that, at least, went as planned.'

Flora stared at her. 'Planned? What are you talking about?'

'Yes.' The Contessa's voice was meditative. 'I am afraid you are quite dense. You see, it was not by chance that you encountered Marco that day. He followed you to the restaurant and staged that little comedy afterwards.' She leaned forward, the cold eyes glinting under their heavy lids. 'Do you know why?'

Flora found suddenly that she couldn't speak. There was a tightness in her chest. She was aware of Tonio's gloating smile. Of the haggard face of the girl by the window, who had turned and was watching her now, the dark eyes burning like live coals.

'Now, tell me, *signorina*, what your *fidanzato* said when he found you with Marco at that hotel? He must have been very angry. Did he try to hit him—make a terrible scene?'

Numbly, Flora shook her head.

'And did that not seem strange—a man you had promised to marry simply allowing a stranger to steal you from him without protest? A stranger who had offered him such a terrible insult?'

'I—I expect he had his reasons.' Flora did not recognise her own voice.

'Yes—he had reasons.' The girl by the window spoke for the first time. Moving stiffly, she walked across the room towards Flora, who forced herself to remain where she was when every instinct was screaming at her to run. 'Shall I tell you what they were?' she went on. 'Shall I explain that as soon as he saw Marco—heard his name— he knew exactly who he was, and why he was there. And he turned away in shame.'

She drew a deep shaking breath. 'Because Cristoforo is a man without truth—without honour.'

Flora had been hanging on to her *sangfroid* by her fingertips, anyway, but now she felt it crumble away completely.

She was stumbling, suddenly, through some bleak wilderness. Her voice seemed to come from a far distance. 'You—know Chris?'

The girl threw back her head. 'He did not tell you about me? I knew he would not—the fool—the coward.' She spat the words, and in spite of herself Flora recoiled a step. 'He did not tell you that we met in the Bahamas, on vacation—that from the moment we saw each other nothing and no one else mattered? That we were lovers—and more than lovers. Because I laid my whole life at his feet.'

Her voice shook with frantic emotion. 'I believed he felt as I did, that we would be together always. He— made me believe that—but he lied. On our last night together—when I offered to return to London with him and confront you with the truth that he no longer cared for you—he pretended surprise. He even laughed. He said that he had no intention of breaking his engagement to you because you suited him, and he did not want a wife who would make too many demands.'

Her shrill laugh was edged with hysteria. 'He said what we had shared was only a diversion—a little holiday romance—and that he regretted it if I—I, Ottavia Baressi—had taken it too seriously.'

She shook her head. 'He was so cruel—cruel beyond belief. He said that the best I could do was forget everything that had passed between us and return to my own *fidanzato*. Get on with my life, as he meant to do—with you.'

She wrapped her arms tightly round her body. 'And when, later, I tried to telephone him in London—to speak to him—to reason with him—he did not want to talk to me.'

Flora said carefully, 'But why should you want to do that? When he'd made his position so clear? Why didn't you put him behind you and try and make your—your engagement work?'

'Because I found I was expecting his child. I thought if he knew that, then he might change—realise that we belonged together.'

Flora felt as if she'd been poleaxed. 'You—were going to have a baby? Then he must have said something.'

All this, she thought, had been going on, and she'd suspected nothing—nothing…

'He was so angry. He shouted at me—called me a liar, and other bad names. Said that I was a *sciattona*—a slut—who slept with any man, and that there was no proof that it was his baby. That he wasn't a fool, and he would fight me in court, if necessary, and make a big scandal. Then he laughed and said, "Or you could always blame Signor Valante and bring the wedding day forward."'

She shuddered. 'He thought I would do that—add to the dishonour I had brought to my family—and to Marco. That was when I knew I would be revenged on him. That I would hurt him and ruin his life, as he had done to me. And, because he had left me to go back to you, I decided you should also know what it is to be betrayed and deserted by a man who has pretended to love you.'

Flora's hands turned into fists, her nails scoring the soft palms as she fought for her last remnants of control.

Her voice was small and cold. 'And—Marco agreed to this? I don't believe you.'

Ottavia's eyes glinted with savage satisfaction. 'No. Just as I did not believe that Cristoforo would ever leave me. We were both wrong, *signorina*. And Mamma is, after all, Marco's *madrina*. In Italy that means a great deal. She made him see that it was his duty to avenge me—and his honour also. And that Cristoforo should know what had been done—and why.' She shrugged almost triumphantly. 'So—he came to find you, Flora Graham. And the rest you know.'

Flora's legs felt so weak she was terrified that they would betray her, and she would end up on the floor at Ottavia's feet. She said, 'You had your revenge, Signorina Baressi, as I'm sure Marco reported to you. Was it really necessary to tell me all this?'

'Yes,' Ottavia threw at her. 'Because Marco was supposed to leave you in London, to count the cost of your lust and stupidity. Instead he brought you here, to his home. And you were not given a guest suite, like any of his other whores. No—you must sleep with him in his own room—in the bed where he was born—and his father and grandfather before him. The place where I, as his wife, should have slept. Ninetta, who used to work for Mamma, has told us everything. No one at San Silvestro can believe he would do such a thing. It has outraged everyone.

'And, now, while he is away, you give orders as if

you were the mistress of the house, instead of just his fancy woman—for whom his fancy seems to be waning. If it ever existed at all,' she added contemptuously.

Flora was shaking so violently inside she thought she would fall to pieces, but she couldn't allow that to happen. Not here. Not yet.

She even managed a note of defiance. 'Why else would I be here?'

The Contessa shrugged. 'Maybe he pities you. Or else is grateful for your unstinting co-operation,' she added with cold mockery. 'Certainly your willingness to share his bed must have amused him, and my godson likes to be entertained. But your usefulness was expended in England. He should never have brought you here.'

'Perhaps you had better tell him so.'

'Oh, we shall have a great deal to say to him,' the Contessa said softly. 'Make no mistake about that, Miss Flora Graham.'

She turned to Tonio. 'Our guest is clearly shocked. Fetch her some brandy.'

Flora shook her head. 'I want nothing. Except to get out of here.'

The Contessa leaned back in her chair, studying Flora from under lowered lids. 'No doubt you are eager to go back to the *castello*—to confront Marco on his return and beg him to tell you that none of this is true. If so, you will be disappointed—and even more humiliated than you are now.'

She paused. 'But there is an alternative.' She snapped her fingers and Tonio hurried to pass her a narrow folder from a nearby table. 'This is a plane ticket to England on a flight that leaves this evening. If you wish to take advantage of it my nephew will drive you to the airport. I shall inform Marco myself that you have learned the truth and returned to London. Once you have gone the whole matter can finally be laid to rest.'

She held out the ticket. 'Take it, *signorina*. Learn sense at last. There is nothing left for you here.'

Flora's instinct was to tear the folder into small pieces and throw them at the Contessa. But she couldn't afford to do that, and she knew it. She'd been offered an escape route and she needed to take it, whatever the cost to her pride.

Except she no longer had any pride. Realising how cruelly and cynically she'd been manipulated had left her self-esteem in tatters. She felt bone-weary, and sick at heart. And too anguished even to cry.

She said tonelessly, 'My clothes—belongings—are still at the *castello*.'

'No, they are here,' the Contessa told her. 'I thought you would see where your best interests lay. I told Ninetta to pack your things and have them brought here. You can leave as soon as you wish.'

Flora lifted her chin. 'The sooner, the better, I think. Don't you?'

'Then—*addio, signorina*.' The thin lips stretched in a chill smile. 'We shall not, I think, meet again. Your involvement in this affair was an unfortunate necessity which is now over.'

'Signorina Flora.' Tonio was at the door, holding it open for her.

As she reached it Flora turned, looking back at Ottavia, studying her frankly voluptuous figure in the pink dress. 'Tell me,' she said. 'What happened to the baby?'

Something fleeting came and went in Ottavia's face, but her voice was haughty. 'I did not choose to have it.

Do you think that a Baressi would give birth to an illegitimate child?'

'After today,' Flora said quietly, 'I would say the
Baressis are capable of anything.'

And, she thought, as the stunned numbness began to
wear off and pain tore at her, so are the Valantes. Oh,
Marco—*Marco*...

She drew a deep, shaky breath, then, without another
word or backward glance, she walked through the dark
hall and out towards the harsh dazzle of sunshine.

The drive to the airport seemed endless. She sat beside
Tonio in a kind of frozen stupor, her hands clasped so
tightly in her lap that her fingers ached, her eyes blind
as she stared through the windscreen ahead of her.

'You are not very amusing, *cara*,' her companion
commented after a few miles.

'I seem to have mislaid my sense of humour.'

He clicked his tongue in reproof. 'You must not
brood, you know, because your little holiday in the sun
has been cut short. We could not allow you to cling to
your illusions any longer, and one day you will be grateful to us.'

'Possibly,' Flora rejoined shortly. 'But forgive me if
I'm not overwhelmed with gratitude at the moment.'

Tonio laughed softly. 'You are not very lucky with
your men, are you, *carissima*? Your *fidanzato* betrays
you and your lover takes you for revenge. It is not a
happy situation for you.'

'It hasn't exactly been a joyous time for your cousin
Ottavia either,' Flora came back at him sharply as she
remembered the fleeting moment of pain and vulnera-
bility that had surfaced among the spite and hysteria.

And she realised with shock that she had barely spared a thought for Chris's behaviour in all this.

'Oh, Ottavia will survive,' he said with insouciance. 'She has the Baressi name and money behind her, after all, and there has been no open scandal. My aunt is a careful woman.'

Flora bit her lip. 'I believe you.'

Tonio lowered his voice confidentially. 'I think she hopes that even now she can persuade Marco to remember the ties between our families and resume his engagement to Ottavia.'

Flora turned her head slowly and stared at him. 'You actually think that—after everything that's happened?'

'Why not?' He shrugged. 'It was not a love match the first time. Marco, you see, does not really care about women. Oh, he likes them as decoration, to be seen with in public, and he enjoys their bodies. But that is all.'

He shrugged again. 'It was time for him to marry, and one woman is very like another to him. That must have been the only reason for his engagement to Ottavia. She is beautiful, certainly, but so demanding.'

She said stonily, 'Then you won't be offering to console her?'

He laughed. 'She has never tempted me. But you, *carissima*, are a different proposition,' he added, giving her a sidelong glance. 'We could always change your air ticket to a later date. Italy has many beauties and I would be happy to be your guide. What do you think?'

'You really don't want to know what I think.' She was suddenly aware that his hand was straying in the direction of her knee, and stiffened. 'And if you lay one finger on me, *signore*, I'll break your jaw.'

He shrugged. 'Well, it is your loss, not mine. But then,

you are a loser all round, Signorina Flora,' he added with a sly smile.

They completed the rest of the journey in silence. When they arrived at the airport Tonio reached into his jacket and produced an envelope which he extended to her.

'What is this?' Flora made no attempt to take it.

'A further gift from my aunt.' He peeled back a corner of the flap, revealing the substantial wad of banknotes inside. 'She is aware that Marco would have been generous with you on parting and does not wish you to suffer financially from her intervention. She offers this as compensation.'

'She's very thoughtful.' Flora opened the passenger door. 'But I'm not for sale.'

Tonio got out as well, and retrieved her bag from the boot. 'Oh, I think you were sold, Flora *mia*,' he said softly. 'And for thirty pieces of silver. *Ciao*, baby.'

As she walked to the glass doors leading to the main concourse she heard him drive away. And then—and only then—she allowed one slow, scalding tear to escape down the curve of her cheek.

'You look terrible,' said Hester, in a tone that mingled brutal candour with concern.

'Thanks for the vote of confidence,' Flora retorted.

'I'm being serious.' Hester poured coffee from the percolator and handed a cup to Flora. 'Ever since you got back from that Italian trip you've looked like death on a stick. You barely ate enough at dinner tonight to keep a fly alive—and not for the first time. If you lose much more weight you'll disappear altogether. And don't think I can't hear you pacing up and down your room every night, when you should be asleep.'

Flora gave her a troubled look. 'Oh, Hes, am I keeping

you awake? I'm so sorry. Maybe it's time I started looking for another place of my own.'

'No, it isn't,' Hester said roundly. 'I prefer to have you here, where I can at least keep a panic-stricken eye on you. But I would like to know what's sent you into this headlong decline.'

Flora stared down at her coffee. She could smell its slightly smoky fragrance and was aware of an odd shiver of distaste.

'It's just frantic at work, that's all,' she evaded. 'Phone ringing non-stop ever since I got back. If it goes on like this I might have to consider hiring someone else.'

'Well, let's hear it for the businesswoman of the year.' Hester gave her a wry look. 'So why aren't you turning cartwheels for joy instead of looking as if ruin and misery were staring you in the face?' She paused, then said gently, 'Be honest, honey. Are you missing Chris—is that it?' She sighed. 'I know I never thought you were the perfect pair, but I wonder now if I didn't push you into doing something you now regret.'

Flora forced a smile. 'I wasn't pushed—I jumped. And I have no regrets at all. I realised that my feelings for Chris were only lukewarm at best, and, anyway, he—wasn't the man I'd believed him to be. End of story.'

'Really?' Hester asked sceptically. 'Somehow I feel I missed out on a few vital episodes, but I won't pry. However, I'd like to know what I can do to help.'

'You've already done it,' Flora said with swift warmth. 'Letting me move in with you while my flat is being sold—and not asking questions,' she added with difficulty.

She wanted to add, 'One day I'll tell you everything,' but she wasn't sure she ever could—not even to Hester, her best friend in the world.

How could she confess to anyone what a monumental, abject fool she'd made of herself? she thought, as she lay awake that night. Let alone admit the even more damaging truth that, try as she might, she was unable to dismiss Marco Valante from her mind and heart?

It was the shame of that knowledge—of the yearning that the mere thought of him could still engender—that pursued her by day and haunted her at night, driving her to walk the floor, fighting the demons of desire that warred within her.

It was nearly six weeks since her headlong flight from Italy, and yet she was no nearer to putting his betrayal in the past, where it belonged, or blocking him from her consciousness.

Each day she'd waited for him to get in touch—to explain the indefensible, or at least apologise. But there had been no contact at all. No letter. No phone call.

Perhaps he'd grown secretly tired of the game he was playing with her, and had been glad of his godmother's intervention.

After the first two weeks of silence she'd taken a cab to his cousin's house in Chelsea, only to find a removals van outside and the new owner's furniture being carried in.

Vittoria, too, had gone. But even if she'd been there, and Flora could have summoned up the courage to introduce herself, what could she have found to say to her? Is Marco well? Is he happy?

And just how pathetic is that? she asked herself with bitter self-derision.

Especially when he seemed to have had no trouble in forgetting her existence altogether.

Her first action on her return had been to put her flat on the market, her next to vacate her rented office space for alternative premises in a different area.

All that trouble to cover her tracks, she thought with irony, when in fact there'd been no need. But she'd had to get out of the flat. She couldn't bear to live with its memories.

She'd found a clutch of increasingly desperate telephone messages from Chris when she returned. Somehow she'd forced herself to dial his number and listen to the impassioned outpourings and demands that they should meet and talk.

At last she'd said, in a voice of quiet steel, 'I think you should be saying this to Ottavia Baressi,' and replaced the receiver, cutting off the ensuing stunned silence.

In spite of Hester's assurances, she knew it was time she started looking for another place to live. Before too long Sally would return and want her room back.

And I have to draw a line under the past and get on with my life, she thought. So I'll take positive action— start flat-hunting tomorrow.

But in the morning she felt so horribly ill that she was more inclined to reserve space in the nearest cemetery.

'It can't be anything I've eaten, because we've had exactly the same and you're fine,' she said as she emerged pale and shivering from the bathroom. 'I must have picked up some virus.'

'Undoubtedly,' Hester agreed cordially. 'I hope you feel better soon.'

And, oddly enough, Flora did. She even recovered sufficiently to go into work, and managed a full day there without further mishap. Although she found herself recoiling from the harmless ham and lettuce sandwich that she'd ordered for her lunch.

'Strange, isn't it?' she commented to Hester that evening.

'Extraordinary.' Hes tossed a bag with a chemist's label into her lap. 'Try this.'

Flora broke the seal and stared down at the slim packet it contained.

She cleared her throat. 'It's a pregnancy testing kit,' she said at last.

'Good,' Hester said affably. 'I was afraid they'd swapped it for a mystery prize. You'll find the instructions inside.'

Flora let the packet fall as if it was red-hot. 'No.'

'As you wish.' Hester shrugged. 'I just thought it was a possibility you might want to eliminate.' She gave her friend a level look. 'Well—don't you?'

'Yes.' Flora bit her lip. 'I suppose so—damn you.'

Even before she checked the result she knew it would be positive. She'd blamed the recent disruption in her monthly cycle on stress, but she knew now she'd simply been burying her head in the sand.

She stared down at the coloured bands on the kit and the bathroom swung round her in a sudden dizzying arc, forcing her to cling to the side of the basin until the moment passed.

She put a hand on her stomach. She thought, Marco's baby. I—I'm going to have Marco's baby... And felt joy and anguish clash inside her with all the force of an electric charge.

Then she opened the door and went slowly back to the living room.

Hester took one look at her white face and trembling mouth, put her into a chair, made her a cup of strong, scalding tea, and stood over her while she drank it.

She said gently, 'I think you'll have to contact Chris, my pet, whether you want to or not.'

'Chris?' Flora looked at her blankly. 'What has Chris got to do with it?' She paused. 'Oh, God, you thought...'

'A reasonable assumption, under the circumstances.' Hester drew up the opposite chair and gave her a searching glance. 'But totally wrong, it seems. I presume you're telling me, instead, that this baby is the result of the torrid affair with your glamorous Italian?' She shook her head. 'I can't believe it. My God, I almost feel sorry for Chris.'

'Then don't,' Flora said with a flash of her old spirit. 'Because I didn't start this. I—I discovered, you see, that Chris had met someone else too, while he was on holiday that time in Bahamas.'

'And you decided what was sauce for the goose?' Hester gave a tuneless whistle. 'Very unwise, my pet.'

'No,' Flora denied tiredly. 'It wasn't like that. I actually only learned about Chris quite a while after—afterwards,' she added, biting her lip.

Hester was silent for a moment. 'Are you going to tell Marco Valante that fatherhood awaits him?'

'There's no point. He doesn't feature in my life any more.' Flora spoke with difficulty, her voice constricted. 'It was a terrible mistake, and—it's over.'

'Not completely,' Hester said bluntly. 'As there are consequences.'

Flora forced a travesty of a smile. 'Only one consequence—I hope. And it's my problem, so I'll deal with it.'

Hester nodded meditatively. 'What are you planning to do? Request a termination?'

Flora had a sudden vision of Ottavia Baressi, struggling to hide a nightmare of pain behind defiant words. Suddenly—defensively—she wrapped her arms round her body, as if protecting the tiny life within her.

How could I possibly do that to Marco's child? she thought with a pang. When it's all I'll ever have of him.

Aloud, she said slowly, 'I know it would be the sensible solution—only I've never been very wise. I can't do it, Hes.'

Her friend frowned. 'Think about it, love,' she urged quietly. 'Yes, you have a career, and a home, so you're better off than a lot of women in your situation. But it still isn't easy trying to bring up a child single-handed. Even with the active support of the father there are all kinds of difficulties.' She hesitated. 'Are you quite sure you won't contact your Italian about all this?'

'No.' Flora shook her head wearily. 'That's quite impossible, and he's not *my* Italian.'

'Whatever, you don't think he has the right to know that you've created a life together?'

'No, he forfeited that—totally.' Flora sent her an appealing look. 'Please don't ask me to explain.'

Hester lifted her hands in a gesture of surrender. 'I'll shut up here and now,' she said. 'But I can think of several people who won't. Starting,' she added gently, 'with your mother.'

'Oh, God,' Flora said wretchedly. 'She's not even speaking to me at the moment as it is.'

'Well, that could be a good thing,' Hester said, straight-faced. 'Keep the fight going and the baby could be in university before she finds out.'

And, in spite of all the fear and misery threatening to crush her, Flora, to her own complete astonishment, found herself giggling weakly.

CHAPTER NINE

FLORA came out of the health centre and stood for a moment, hunting in her bag for her sun glasses. The noise of the city traffic hurtling past was deafening, but she was oblivious to it, locked in her own private world.

Because there was no mistake. It was all true.

Her doctor had just confirmed that her pregnancy test had been totally accurate, and, once Flora's resolve to have the baby had been established, had dealt briskly with the practicalities. Her medical insurance would secure her a bed in a good, private maternity clinic, and she would be contacted in the next few days by the practice midwife who would monitor her well-being in the coming months.

He had also assured her that the sickness that assailed her each morning would probably pass within a month or two.

Tactfully, the doctor had not probed, nor attempted to raise any of the other issues surrounding the coming baby, and Flora was grateful for that.

Her mind was still reeling from the knowledge that Marco's child was growing inside her. She had to come to terms with that before she could cope with anything else, however pressing.

And there were matters to be dealt with. The estate agent had contacted her two days earlier to say that he'd received an offer of the full asking price for her flat, and that the couple concerned were also interested in buying some of the furniture, if she wanted to sell.

'And do you?' Hester asked.

'I think so,' Flora said slowly. 'It might be good to clear my decks—start again from scratch.' She grimaced. 'After all, I'm not looking for a showcase for my career any more, but a family home.'

'Wow,' said Hester. She paused. 'You're really taking this in your stride, honey.'

Perhaps that was because having a baby was small potatoes compared with some of the shocks she'd experienced recently, Flora thought wryly.

She forced a smile. 'It's all front. Underneath, I'm really a quivering mass of insecurity.'

But the sale of the flat was a positive step, and, hopefully, the bed might be included in the furniture that the Morgans wanted to buy. Because there was no way that Flora could have ever spent another night in it, even though it was probably where the baby had been conceived.

After that first incredible, rapturous night, Marco, she remembered, had always been careful to use protection.

As an afterthought, she told herself bitterly, it had been an abject failure.

She glanced at her watch, then walked to the kerb and hailed a passing cab. The agent had suggested it might be simpler if she and Mrs Morgan handled the sale of the furniture between them, and she'd reluctantly agreed, so they were meeting there that morning.

She'd listed the flat's contents, and pencilled in realistic asking prices alongside the main items, making a separate note of the few personal things she intended to keep and which Hester was going to help her remove.

Get it over and done with, she thought as she gave the flat's address to the driver. And then I can move on—make some real plans. Adjust and compromise.

Maybe find somewhere with enough space to enable me to work from home.

She had mixed feelings as she unlocked the door and let herself in. This had been so much her own individual space, yet now it only seemed to speak to her of Marco.

Chris had spent far more time there, but he'd never stamped his personality on the place in the way Marco had done in a few brief hours.

He seemed to be everywhere, sliding his arms round her waist in the kitchen and nuzzling her neck, sharing the narrow bath, sprawling on the sofa with his head in her lap. And, of course, making love to her with heart-stopping skill in the bedroom.

Making himself quite effortlessly part of her environment, she thought with a gasp of sheer pain. And completely essential to her life and happiness.

God, but he'd been clever. Or had she been just a pitiable fool, wanting so hard to believe in the fairy tale?

Whatever, she was older and wiser now, she told herself with determination. And the life and happiness she'd envisaged would have to take a wholly different form.

Her answering machine was blinking, and she frowned as she pressed the 'Play' button. Most people now contacted her through work, but there were bound to be a few who'd slipped through the net.

I'll have to make another list, she thought, sighing, as she retrieved her notebook from her bag. And ask Mrs Morgan if she wants the line to be transferred.

There were only three calls—the first from a girlfriend who'd only just heard about her broken engagement and clearly wanted all the gory details. The second was from her stepsister, furiously demanding to know if she'd come to her senses yet and who was going to pay for the page boy suit.

And the third, inevitably, was from Chris, in a new role as the voice of sweet reason, suggesting that they'd both behaved very badly but that he, at least, was prepared to let bygones be bygones and try again.

Flora listened to it, open-mouthed at his sheer effrontery, then stabbed at the 'Delete' button, nearly breaking a nail in the process.

Somehow, she thought grimly, she was going to have to convince him not to contact her ever again.

She'd assumed her mention of Ottavia would be enough to keep him away, but clearly he was experiencing a sense of decency by-pass.

She was still seething when the doorbell rang, and had to hurriedly arrange her face into more tranquil and pleasant lines as she went to answer its summons. After all, she didn't want to send the unknown Mrs Morgan fleeing in fright down the street, she thought, as she flung open the door.

And stopped, her smile freezing on her lips, her senses screaming into shock, as she saw who was waiting for her.

'*Buongiorno,*' said Marco.

The sound of his voice with its familiar husky note roused her from her sudden stupor. She grabbed at the door, intending to slam it in his face, but he was too fast for her, and too strong. She'd forgotten the deceptive muscularity of the lean body under those elegant suits.

He simply walked past her into the entrance hall. 'Now you may close the door,' he said softly.

'Get out of here. Get out—now.' Her voice cracked in the middle. 'Or I'll call the police—tell them you forced your way in...'

'With no evidence?' he asked crushingly. 'I think not.

And then I shall tell them it is just a lovers' quarrel, and we will see which of us they believe.'

'You can't stay,' Flora said rapidly. 'I'm expecting a visitor…' She paused, her eyes flying to his face with sudden suspicion. 'Or am I?' She drew a deep breath. 'My God, I don't believe this. You've caught me again in the same trap. The flat isn't sold at all, is it? It's just another trick, and the Morgans probably don't even exist.'

'They are quite real, and they are genuinely buying your flat,' Marco returned. 'But not, unfortunately, the furniture. We stretched the truth about that.'

'"We"?' Flora echoed derisively. 'Surely a practised liar like you, *signore*, doesn't need an accomplice.'

He said slowly, 'If you are hoping you will goad me into losing my temper and walking out, you will be disappointed. I came here to talk to you, Flora *mia*, and I shall not leave until I have done so.' He paused. 'But not in this hallway. Let us go into your sitting room.'

Flora did not budge. 'You can talk,' she said clearly. 'But I don't have to listen.'

The green eyes glinted at her. 'Do not put me to the trouble of fetching you, *mia cara*.'

Her hesitation was only momentary. Fetching meant touching, and an instinct older than the world told her that, as long as she lived, she would never be ready to feel his hands on her again.

Skirting round him with minute care, she walked into the living room and went to stand by the window, her arms folded defensively across her body.

Marco propped himself in the doorway, his expression unreadable as he looked her over.

He said, 'You are thinner.'

Flora bit her lip, staring down at the gleaming boards.

'Please don't concern yourself,' she said. 'Because the situation is purely temporary, I assure you.' And could have wept with the terrible irony of it all.

'Have you been ill?'

'No, I've just had a check-up and I'm in excellent health.' She lifted her chin and faced him defiantly. 'I'm sorry if you thought I'd be wasting away—or suicidal. What a blow to your male pride to find me simply— getting on with my life.'

'Why did you decide to sell the flat?'

She shrugged. 'The blank canvas didn't seem appropriate any more.' She paused. 'Is this all you want to ask? Why didn't you get your private detective to submit a questionnaire, and I could have ticked the right boxes?'

'A box would not have told me how angry you are with me.'

'No, but it would have spared me this meeting.' She shook her head. 'Why have you come here? You must have known I would never want to see you again.'

'Yes,' he acknowledged quietly. 'I was afraid it would be so. Which was why I delayed my journey. I hoped, if I gave you time, you might, in turn, allow me the opportunity to explain.'

'That's unnecessary. Your godmother supplied all the explanation I could ever need. I know everything, *signore*, so you may as well go back where you came from.'

'You are determined not to listen to me,' he said slowly. 'Even after all we have been to each other.'

'I know what you once were to me,' Flora said bitingly. 'Thanks to the Contessa, I'm now aware of all I was to you. There's nothing more to be said.'

'There is a great deal more,' he snapped. 'And I was coming back from Milan to say it to you—to tell you everything. To confess and ask your forgiveness. Only to find you had gone and all hell had broken loose.'

'Oh, please.' To her fury, she realised she was trembling. 'Am I really supposed to believe that?' She shook her head. 'Don't tell me any more of your lies, Marco. I won't be made a fool of a second time.'

'No,' he said bitterly. 'I am the one who has been a fool—and worse than a fool. What point is there in pretending otherwise?'

'None at all,' she said. 'But pretending is what you do best, *signore*, and old habits die hard.'

He said slowly, 'While we are on the subject of pretence, *signorina*, do you intend to maintain that you did not expect me to come after you? And that there is nothing left in your heart of that passion—the need that we shared?'

'Your conceit, Signor Valante, is only matched by your arrogance.' Flora's voice sparked with anger.

'That is no answer.'

'It's the only one you're going to get,' she flashed.

His laugh was husky, almost painful. 'Then I will ask another question. Flora—will you be my wife?'

The world suddenly seemed to lurch sideways. There was a strange roaring in her ears and she saw the floor rising to meet her.

When awareness slowly returned, she found she was lying on the sofa and Marco was kneeling beside her, holding a glass of water.

'Drink this,' he directed shortly, and she complied unwillingly. He watched her, his mouth drawn into a grim, straight line.

He said, 'And you say you are not sick.'

'I'm not.' Flora handed back the glass and sat up gingerly. 'I had a shock, that's all.'

'Is it really so shocking to receive a proposal of marriage?'

'From you—yes.' She could taste the sourness of tears in her throat. 'But then why should I really be surprised? It's time you were married, isn't it? And one woman is as good as any other. I'm told that's your philosophy. Be honest, *signore*.'

He was silent for a long moment. 'It may have been—once. God forgive me. But not now.'

'So, what is it this time?' Flora stared at him, her eyes hard. 'A belated attempt to salve your guilty conscience? To offer some recompense for the way you treated me?'

'I want you,' he said quietly. 'And I swore I would move heaven and earth to get you back.'

'Except you don't really believe you'll have to go to those lengths,' she threw at him. 'Not when I was such a push-over the first time around.' She gestured wildly. 'You think you have only to smile, and take my hand— and I'll follow you anywhere. But not this time, *signore*. Because I'm not playing your game any more. I've changed, and I tell you this—I'd rather die than have you touch me—you bastard.'

There was another tingling silence, then Marco said, 'Ah,' and got to his feet. The dark face was cool, composed, and the green eyes steady as they met hers.

He said, 'Then I agree with you, Flora *mia*. There is no more to be said, and I will leave you in peace to enjoy your life.'

As he turned to walk to the door the telephone rang suddenly.

He checked. 'Do you wish me to answer that for you?'

'The machine will pick up the message.' She hardly recognised her own voice. She felt as if she'd been left dying on some battlefield. As perhaps she had.

There was a click, and a woman's voice, clear and pleasant, filled the room. 'This is Barbara Wayne, Miss Graham, the midwife from the health centre. Dr Arthur asked me to contact you and arrange a preliminary appointment. Perhaps you'd call me back and suggest a convenient time—early next week, say? Thank you.'

Flora sat as if she'd been turned to stone, listening to the tape switch off and run back. Her mouth was bone-dry and her heart was beating an alarmed tattoo against her ribcage. She did not dare look at Marco, but the words of the message seemed to hang in the room.

Useless to hope that he had not picked up its exact implication.

If it had just been five minutes later, she thought, fighting back a sob of desperation. Just five minutes... He would have been gone. And she would have been safe. Whereas now...

When he eventually spoke, his tone was almost remote. The polite interest of a stranger. 'Is it true? Are you carrying my child?'

She set her teeth to stop them chattering. 'What— makes you think it's yours?'

'Now who is playing games?' There was a note under the surface of his voice that made her shiver. 'Do not prevaricate—or lie to me. Are you having our baby?'

She closed her eyes. 'Yes.'

'At last, some honesty.' There was another terrible silence, then he sighed. 'Well, even if I am a bastard, as you say, Flora *mia*, I will not allow my child to be born as one. You and I will be married as soon as it can be arranged.'

'No.' She was on her feet. 'I won't do it. You can't make me.'

He smiled grimly. 'I think I can, *mia bella*. You have

made it clear you find me repulsive.' He shrugged. 'I can accept that. But our child will be born within the protection of marriage.' His voice hardened. 'What happens afterwards will be a matter for negotiation, but it will not include the usual demands a husband makes of his wife.'

'To hell with your negotiations.' Flora was shaking. 'I still say no.'

'You wish to give up the baby?' Marco asked coldly. 'Or do you want me to fight you for custody through the courts, with all the attendant lurid publicity that will entail? Because I guarantee you will lose.'

'You can't say that.' The breath caught in her throat. 'Judges favour mothers.'

'Not always. And can you afford the risk—or the cost of a long legal war?' His smile froze her. 'I do not think so.'

He paused. 'But, if you marry me, I promise complete financial support for you and the baby in return for proper visitation rights. I shall not even require you to live under my roof after the birth,' he added drily. 'And in time we can divorce discreetly.'

There was a terrible tightness in her chest, as if someone had grasped her heart and was squeezing out every last drop of blood.

She said thickly, 'You've betrayed me once. Why should I trust you this time?'

His mouth curled. 'Because I don't bed unwilling women, *cara*. As my wife, and the mother of my child, you will receive my respect, but nothing more.' He paused, his gaze faintly mocking. 'Do you want my lawyers to draw up a written assurance?'

'No.' She bit her lip. 'That—won't be necessary.'

'Do I take it, then, that you agree to my terms?'

She said, dully, 'I don't seem to have a great deal of choice.'

'Then you may choose now. Do you wish a large wedding or a small one?'

'A small one,' she said. 'And as quiet as possible.' She lifted her chin. 'I'm not proud of what I'm doing.'

'It is not what I would wish either,' Marco said quietly. 'But we must consider what is best for the child we have made together.'

She walked over to the window and stood, staring unseeingly at the street. 'Have you thought of what your godmother will say about this?'

He said curtly, 'Her views are of no concern to me. In any case, she is giving up the villa and returning to Rome, so you will not be obliged to meet with her again.'

She said with difficulty, 'But you—do expect me to live at the *castello*?'

'It is a tradition for Valante children to be born there—as I am sure you already know.' His tone was brusque.

Yes, she thought, with a stab of anguish. In that big canopied bed in the tower, where we were lovers...

Dear God, I can't bear it—I *can't*...

She didn't look at him. 'I presume you will be spending most of your time in Milan?'

'Naturally,' he said drily. 'I would not be the first husband to use work as an excuse to keep his distance. Although not usually so early in the marriage.'

'No,' she said. 'I—I suppose not.'

She kept her back turned because she dared not—*dared* not—face him. Because he might look into her eyes and see all the confusion of misery and yearning that was suddenly rising inside her in spite of herself.

And she knew if he came to her, and took her in his arms, she would be lost for ever. She could not take that risk.

He said suddenly, 'Your friend Hester. How much have you told her?'

'Just that I had a stupid, dangerous affair, and am now pregnant as a result.' She spoke defiantly. How silly, she thought, to have imagined that there was anywhere she could go where he wouldn't find her exactly when he wished. 'I also said that I wanted nothing more to do with you, so I shall have some explaining to do.'

'I am sure you will make your—change of heart convincing,' he said softly. 'Do you wish her to be a witness at our wedding?'

She forced a smile. 'I don't think I could keep her away if I tried.'

'Perhaps you should let me talk to her, so that I can reassure her that this marriage is in everyone's best interests.' He hesitated. 'Will you both have dinner with me at my hotel this evening?'

'Thank you,' she said. 'But that—won't be necessary.' She steadied her voice. 'I've agreed to go through a wedding ceremony with you. Let that be enough.'

He said icily, 'As you wish. I will contact you, then, only when the arrangements are made.'

'I think it would be better,' she said, then weakened her position by adding, 'If you don't mind.'

'Why should I mind? As you reminded me, *cara*, I

am a philosopher, and one woman is like any other. I will try not to forget again.'

His tone was sardonic. 'However, I should warn you that my respect for you as my wife will not necessarily guarantee my fidelity. I do not intend to be lonely, although I shall be discreet. I trust you can accept that?'

'Of course.' Her voice was barely audible.

'Good.' He sounded almost brisk. 'Then I will leave you in peace, as you desire. *Arriverderci*, Flora *mia*.'

She heard him leave the room, and, presently, the sound of the front door closing.

She made her way slowly to the sofa and sank down on its cushions. Well, she had managed to keep him at a serious distance, she thought, and, under the circumstances, that was a personal triumph. So why did she feel as if she'd suffered a crushing defeat instead?

I do not intend to be lonely. The words reverberated over and over in her mind, creating images she did not wish to contemplate.

Especially when it seemed she had condemned herself to an agony of loneliness for the rest of her life.

She drew a deep, shuddering breath. Well, she had done what she had to do—if she was to preserve her self-respect—and her sanity.

And now—somehow—she had to live with the consequences.

Hester was hovering, her eyes alive with curiosity, when Flora got home that evening.

'So,' she said. 'Why are we too busy to have dinner with Marco Valante tonight?'

Flora gasped. 'How do you know about that?'

'Because he phoned about half an hour ago to express his regrets and say that the invitation was still open.' She glanced at her watch. 'And, as he doesn't sound like the kind of guy who takes rejection well, that gives us just over an hour to glam up and get there.'

Flora became a living statue. 'No,' she said baldly.

'Is that a real no? Or an "I could be persuaded in the fullness of time" job?'

'A real no,' Flora said hotly. 'Oh, how dare he?'

Hester shrugged. 'Presumably because he wants company at dinner?'

Flora shook her head. 'It's really not as simple as that.'

'Then tell me about it,' said Hester. 'You have my undivided attention. And I already know that he's undoubtedly the baby's father, so you can skip that bit.'

Flora took a deep breath. 'We're going to be married.'

'Right,' Hester said evenly, after a minute. 'When was this decision made?'

'Today. He—just turned up. Unexpectedly,' she added with constraint.

'Good choice of word,' Hester approved affably. 'Because I have the feeling I've just stepped into a parallel universe here. Or was it some other man you were swearing you never wanted to see again only twenty-four hours ago?'

'I didn't—and I don't. But he's found out about the baby and he refuses to allow it to be born illegitimate.'

She paused. 'So we made a deal—marriage in return for financial support and reasonable access.'

Hester gave her a long look. 'This sounds more like a business arrangement than a relationship.'

'Yes,' said Flora. 'That's exactly what it is—and nothing more.'

There was a loaded silence, then Hester said carefully, 'May I just recap here? I've known you for years, Flo, and you're not the promiscuous kind. You never have been. But this is the man for whom you suddenly and spectacularly dumped Chris, remember? Not only that but you allowed this Marco Valante to sweep you off and have unprotected sex with you. He's made you act completely out of character ever since you met, so ''business arrangement'' hardly covers it.'

'And I told you that the whole thing was a disastrous mistake.' Flora made herself meet her friend's concerned gaze. 'On both sides,' she added. 'So we're just trying to make the best of a bad job.'

'But all this civilised behaviour doesn't include having dinner with the guy?' Hester shook her head. 'It sounds to me as if you're running scared, Flo.'

There was another taut silence, then Flora sighed defeatedly. 'Very well, then. Call him back and tell him we'll be there. I presume he's staying at the Mayfair Tower?'

'You know he is.' Hester gave her a swift hug. 'Besides, the food there is bound to be better than the ham salad we had planned—especially when you're eating for two now,' she added slyly.

Flora gave her a constrained smile. 'Please don't remind me.'

Marco was waiting for them in the bar, meeting Flora's fulminating look with equanimity and no overt air of triumph.

Hester was wary to begin with, but was soon blinking under the full force of his charm.

He was relaxed, amusing and attentive to Flora, without undue fuss. And, apart from offering her his arm as they went into the dining room, he was scrupulous about avoiding physical contact with her.

He should have been an actor, Flora thought sourly as she sipped her sole glass of vintage champagne.

But she couldn't fault him as a host, and the food and wine were delicious.

The only awkward moment occurred at the end of the evening, when he was seeing them to a waiting taxi. Acutely aware of Hester's expectant gaze, Flora allowed him to take her hand and kiss it.

He said softly, 'I'll call you tomorrow, *carissima*,' and bent to kiss her cheek.

It was the merest brush of his lips, but her whole body surged in a response of such force that she nearly cried out.

She murmured something, then stepped back, avoiding his gaze.

'So,' Hester said, as they drove home. 'You still maintain this marriage is just a business arrangement?'

'Yes,' Flora said defensively. 'What of it?'

Hester shrugged. 'Just that, when questioned, nine out of ten women said that, given the chance, they'd rip his clothes off and drag him into bed. And the tenth was in her nineties and short-sighted.'

She groaned. 'God, Flo, he exudes sex like lesser men do aftershave. I felt it when I first saw him and it wasn't even directed at me. Also, he's seriously rich and definitely powerful. So—why the arm's length treatment? Are you completely mad?'

'I certainly was,' Flora returned shortly. 'Which is why I'm in this appalling mess now. And I'm not going down that path again. Ever.' She hesitated. 'I do have my reasons, Hes.'

'Then I have to admire your will-power, even if I don't understand it.' Hester took her hand and gave it a comforting squeeze. 'And I wish you luck, honey, because something tells me that you're absolutely going to need it.'

And as she lay awake that night, trying unsuccessfully to ignore the demands of her unsatisfied body, Flora was forced to concede unhappily that Hester could well be right.

CHAPTER TEN

THE ring was plain, gold, unflashy and made no overt statement, but each time Flora moved her hand she was acutely aware of its presence—and its significance.

She was now Marco's wife, legally if in no other way.

And she had to admit reluctantly that so far he had kept his word unfalteringly about that.

She had dreaded that on her arrival at the *castello* she would be expected to occupy the tower rooms again, even if she did sleep there alone, but to her relief she had been given another suite on the opposite side of the building, large and airy and decorated in light pastels.

'You may, of course, change anything you wish,' Marco had said courteously as she'd looked over her new surroundings.

'It's totally charming. I wouldn't want to alter a thing,' Flora had returned with equal politeness.

But it had been a tricky moment, because Marco had reacted with surprising heat when Flora had refused point-blank to sell her business.

'I've worked hard to build it up.' She'd faced him defiantly. 'And I can keep in touch on an everyday basis via the internet. I intend to fly home once a month for consultancy purposes.'

He was frowning darkly. 'Is that wise—when you are pregnant?'

'I'm perfectly fit,' she said. 'And anyway, it's not up for negotiation. I'm going to need my job to go back to—later.'

A muscle flickered at the side of his mouth. He said coolly, 'There is no need for you to work again. I have said I will make financial arrangements for you and the child.'

Flora lifted her chin. 'All the same, I love my job, and I prefer to maintain my independence. Also I've managed to find additional help, so I shan't have to knock myself out in the coming months.'

During the inevitable flurry of preparations for the wedding she'd heard on the grapevine that a young designer called Jane Allen was looking for a change of scene. Flora had met her, liked her immediately, established it was mutual, and that she would frankly relish being flung in at the deep end, and signed her up on the spot.

But Marco, she knew, had not been appeased in the slightest.

On a happier note, she had been touched by the warmth of her reception at the *castello*. All the staff from Alfredo downwards seemed genuinely pleased by her return as the Signora.

She'd been agreeably surprised to discover that Ninetta had gone, along with her brother, and presumably was now in Rome with the Contessa, so that particular fly had been removed from the ointment.

And it saved me having to fire her, Flora thought grimly.

When she was subjected to some very obvious cossetting, she realised resignedly that the staff had guessed with the speed of light why their young mistress was sometimes unwell in the mornings.

She also discovered that the Signore's decision to sleep alone was regarded as a sign of his concern for his bride's fragile health so early in her pregnancy. Not all men, it was hinted, were so kind or considerate at such a delicate time.

Saint Marco, thought Flora, concealing her gritted teeth under a dulcet smile.

But she could hardly complain that he was adhering so strictly to the terms of the deal, after she'd made it abundantly clear that she wanted him nowhere near her, she reminded herself unhappily.

Except that she was lonely. She was surrounded by devoted people, but she realised immediately that the *castello* was only really alive when Marco came back from Milan at the weekend.

And it was hard to remain aloof—to mirror his cool courtesy—when she longed to run to him and fling herself into his arms on his return.

He had suggested once that she might wish to invite her family to stay with her, but Flora had not taken up the idea. Her mother had reacted badly to news of the wedding, and had refused point-blank to attend. She was still convinced that Marco was connected with the Mafia, and prophesied nothing but doom and disaster. And Flora knew of old that where she led the rest of the family would follow.

The good news, however, was that Hester had holiday left, and was coming to stay in the autumn.

In the meantime, being pampered in the lap of luxury and discreetly coached in the management of a large household by Alfredo and his wife was hardly the worst fate that could have befallen her.

And if she kept repeating that to herself, she might, eventually, come to believe it, she thought, sighing.

Gradually she was noticing her body changing, adapting lushly to its new role, and the eminent gynaecologist that

Marco had engaged to look after her expressed complete satisfaction with her progress.

He also mentioned discreetly that now the pregnancy was firmly established the Signora could happily resume marital relations with her husband, and went away thinking sentimentally how charming it was that his latest patient should blush so deeply at such an ordinary suggestion.

The truth was that Flora was fighting a bitter war with herself—her emotions locked in mortal combat with her common sense.

Marco had claimed he'd come to find her because he wanted her, but he had never, even in their most passionately intimate moments, said that he loved her.

And desire, however strong, was such a transient thing, she told herself, troubled. It took far more than that to make a marriage, especially when the female half was on the verge of swelling up like a barrage balloon. That needed the kind of love she would sell her soul for.

And, since she'd arrived at the *castello*, Marco had never given the slightest hint by word or sign that he'd been tempted to break his self-imposed rules. On the contrary, she acknowledged with a faint sigh.

Which could indicate that only his weekends with her were celibate. That during his working week in Milan he had already found someone else to share his nights.

And that meant that all Flora had to offer him was the tiny human being growing inside her. Once she'd given birth she would be totally surplus to requirements.

The realisation was preying on her mind—driving her crazy.

She should be relaxed and tranquil, as the consultant had told her, and instead she was being torn apart by misery and the kind of jealousy she had never dreamed could exist.

As a consequence, when he was at the *castello* she heard her voice becoming clipped and cool, knew that her body language was guarded and even hostile.

Because she was already preparing herself for the pain of parting. Armouring herself against a hurt that would be as damaging as it was inevitable.

At the same time she was fighting a real sense of shame that she could feel all this for a man who had taken and used her only to fuel his need for revenge. A man she had tried so hard to hate.

Oh, why couldn't he have just left her and gone once he'd achieved his purpose? she thought in anguish. Why had he brought her to his home—and allowed her to fall deeply and irrevocably in love with him?

And, once the truth was out, why couldn't he have left her alone to recover from the trauma of it in peace? Instead, he had condemned her to this half-life, and she wasn't sure how much she could take.

Her trips back to London were only a passing distraction, too, she'd discovered. Business was good, clients were plentiful, and Jane was running the company with flair. So much so that Flora wasn't sure she was really needed there either, and knew that sooner or later Jane was going to offer to buy her out.

I'm going to be like a stateless person, she thought.

When Hester came to stay she wasn't alone. She was accompanied by Andrew, who was tall, brown-haired and humorous, and who looked at Hester so adoringly that Flora felt a lump in her throat. Her wary wise-cracking friend was suddenly transformed into a woman with a dream in her eyes and a smile of pure fulfilment curving her lips.

And Flora hated herself for feeling envious in the face of their obvious joy.

'The wedding's going to be in the late spring,' Hester confided. 'By which time the baby will be here, and you can wear something glamorous as matron of honour.'

'It's a date.' Flora kept her smile pinned in place, and perhaps Hes noticed, because she gave her a swift hug.

'How are things?' she whispered. 'I must say Marco's the perfect host.'

'Everything's fine,' Flora returned.

It was while she was waving them goodbye that she was conscious for the first time of a faint fluttering like a tiny bird in her abdomen.

'Oh.' She touched herself with a questioning hand.

'Is something wrong?' Marco's tone was sharp.

'No.' She marshalled a smile. 'On the contrary. I think the baby just moved.'

He took a half-step towards her, his hand going out, then stopped, the dark face closing over.

He said quietly, 'That is—wonderful news. But I hope you will not become too uncomfortable.'

'No,' she said, choking back the threatened tears of disappointment. 'I—I gather that can happen.' She gave him a brief, meaningless smile, and went back into the *castello*. By the time she came down to dinner he was already on his way back to Milan.

As her body had swelled she'd been glad to see the end of the intense heat of summer, although she missed her daily gentle swim. Autumn at the *castello* was cool and rainy, and she walked every day instead.

On one of her forays she found a small terrier dog of indeterminate breed crouching miserably under a tree, and coaxed him to follow her home. He wasn't received with unmixed joy by the staff.

'He is a stray, *signora*. He could be diseased,' Alfredo told her, concerned.

'Then ask the vet to come and look him over.' Flora stroked the small shaggy head with a gentle hand. 'I wonder where he came from?'

Alfredo pursed his lips. 'From one of the rented villas, *signora*. People do not always take their animals home after a holiday.'

'How vile,' Flora said with some heat. 'Anyway, he'll be company for me. And he'll be fine once he's had a bath and something to eat.'

Alfredo went off muttering, but by the time the little dog had been vetted and groomed he looked altogether more respectable, and, after only a few days, felt so much at home that an armchair in the *salotto* had become his designated abode.

'And we will see what the Signore has to say about that,' Alfredo said ominously.

But Marco seemed merely amused. 'You should have said you wanted a dog, *cara*,' he remarked, fondling the little animal's pointed ears and receiving an adoring look in return that made Flora silently grind her teeth. 'I would have found you a pedigree litter to choose from.'

'Thank you,' Flora said politely. 'But I think dogs pick their owners, and I prefer my little mutt.'

And Mutt he was, from then on.

But, as an apparent consequence of his introduction into the household, Marco started staying in Milan for the weekends too, confirming Flora's unhappy conviction that he had a mistress there.

But he was at home for Christmas and New Year, which were celebrated quietly, although Alfredo had told her that there had often been large parties in the past.

'But they are a lot of work, *signora*,' he said. 'And

the Signore will be anxious that you do not become overtired.'

Perhaps, thought Flora. Or more likely he did not wish to introduce his temporary wife to his family and friends when he knew it would be the only Christmas she would spend at the *castello*.

Her gift from Marco came in a flat velvet case. One perfect pearl, like a captured tear on its thin gold chain, she thought as he fastened it round her throat, her body shivering in involuntary delight as his fingers brushed briefly against her skin.

In her turn, she'd been careful to avoid anything too overtly personal and gave him a tall, frighteningly expensive crystal decanter that she'd found in an antique shop on her last visit to London.

And he thanked her with a smile that did not reach his eyes.

The weather turned much colder in January, and although Flora still took Mutt for his daily run, she did not go so far afield. She found she tired easily these days, especially as the baby was particularly active at night. Like a drum being beaten from the inside, she thought, remembering a line from a Meryl Streep movie she'd once seen.

Sometimes the movements were clearly visible, and she was aware of Marco watching her one evening, as she lay on the sofa, his attention frowningly absorbed on the tiny kicks and thumps that rippled the cling of her dress.

Do you want to touch? she longed to say. Do you want to feel how it feels?

But then he got up abruptly from his chair and went to his study to work, and the moment passed, unshared.

There was a small shop selling delectable babywear in one of the streets off the town square, and Flora was a regular visit every time new stock came in.

One day, as she emerged with her latest purchases, she realised she was being watched, and, looking round, saw Ninetta standing on the opposite side of the street, staring at her.

She half lifted a hand, but the other woman ducked her head and scuttled away.

She mentioned the encounter casually to Alfredo as he drove her home.

'The Contessa Baressi's villa has been sold, *signora*. I think some members of the family have come down to remove their personal possessions.'

'Oh.' Her tone was subdued.

'But have no fear, *signora*,' he added reassuringly. 'The Signore's orders are clear, and even if they call at the *castello* they will not be admitted.'

Mutt was waiting for her at the door, tail wagging furiously.

'All right, old boy.' Flora bent with difficulty to pat him. 'I'll take you out now. Fetch his leash for me, will you, Alfredo?'

'Do you think that is wise, *signora*?' He peered at the sky. 'It will be dark soon.'

'I won't go far,' she promised.

The wind was cold on the coast road, and she walked as quickly as she could, her head bent, while Mutt pranced eagerly ahead of her in the rapidly fading light.

Traffic was almost non-existent in winter, and she frowned as she heard the sound of a car approaching fast. She whistled to Mutt, who came running, and clipped on his lead. As she straightened she was caught in the beam of headlights, and flung up a hand to shield her eyes. She expected the car to pull over, but it seemed to be coming straight for her, and she cried out, throwing herself desperately to one side, fleetingly aware of a face, framed in a mass of dark hair, in the driving seat.

She fell heavily, and felt the fume-filled draught on her face as the car went past, its tyres screaming on the wet surface of the road. Mutt, barking hysterically, tried to chase after it, but fortunately she had his lead twisted round her wrist, and after a few abortive attempts to free himself he trotted back and licked her face.

Flora lay very still, her cheek pressed against damp freezing turf, all her senses at fever pitch as she tried to assess what damage might have been done.

Kick me, she pleaded silently to the baby. Kick me hard. But nothing happened.

When, eventually, she tried to move, she felt her ankle screaming at her to stop, and lay back again. She knew she needed to stay calm, but as the minutes passed she began to feel chilled and also extremely scared.

The driver of the car must have seen her fall, she thought in shocked bewilderment, but had made no attempt to stop even though it must have been obvious that she was heavily pregnant.

How long would it be before she was missed at the *castello*? And, when she was, how would they know which direction she had taken?

She swallowed convulsively. 'Oh, Mutt,' she whispered. 'I think I could be in real trouble.'

As if in confirmation, Mutt flattened his ears, threw back his head, and began to howl.

Time became a blur of cold, and thin rain, and Mutt's distress. She tried several times to get up, but the pain in her ankle invariably sent her wincing back to the ground. She was sure it wasn't broken, but it could be badly sprained, which was just as inconvenient.

She became aware that she was drifting in and out of consciousness, and knew that this was the biggest danger. Mutt was quiet too, as if he'd decided his efforts were in vain, and she loosened his lead and whispered, 'Home, boy,' praying that the sight of him would speed up the search.

Unless, of course, he got sidetracked by a stray cat, or some other legitimate prey, she thought as she heard him in the distance, bursting into a frenzy of excited barking.

But that wasn't the only noise. There were voices, she realised, and bobbing lights.

Or was she just delirious with the cold and imagining it all?

Because it seemed as if Marco was beside her, his voice saying brokenly, 'Flora—*mia carissima*. Ah, *Dio*, my angel, my sweet love. What has happened to you?'

She knew that was impossible, because Marco was miles away in Milan, and anyway he didn't care about her enough to say things like that.

Only his arms were strong around her, and she was breathing the familiar scent of his skin, listening to him murmuring the endearments in his own language that he had once whispered to her when they were making love. And somehow this surpassed every moment of rapture she had ever known with him.

But as he tried to lift her she cried out, 'My ankle,' and fell back alone into the darkness.

When she opened her eyes again there was light so bright that it was almost painful. And there was a soft mattress under her aching body, a sharp hospital smell in the air, and tight strapping round her throbbing ankle.

There was also Marco, his face haggard, until he turned into a bearded man in a white coat, who smiled kindly and asked how she felt.

'Like one big bruise,' she said, her voice husky. And then, with sudden fear, 'My baby?'

'Still in place, Signora Valante, and waiting for a proper birthday. You are a strong lady, and your child is strong too.'

'Thank God,' she whispered, and lay back against the pillow, tears trickling down her face. When she could speak, she said, 'I thought—my husband...'

'He is here, *signora*. I will let you talk to him, then you must rest, and in the morning, if all is well, he can take you home.'

'Everything will be,' she said.

'But first I must ask what happened to you. How you came to be lying by the road in such weather.'

She frowned, trying to remember. 'There was a car,' she said slowly. 'Going too fast. I tried to get out of the way, and fell.'

'Do you know what kind of car—or did you see the number plate?'

She shook her head. 'It all happened so fast.'

'Then we must thank God it was not worse,' he said gravely, and left her.

When she opened her eyes again, Marco was sitting by the bed.

He said hoarsely, 'I thought I had lost you, my love, my dearest heart. *Santa Madonna*, I was so frightened. When I saw you lying there on the grass...'

'But I'm safe,' she told him softly. 'And your baby is safe too.' She pushed aside the covers and took his hand, placing it under the hospital gown on the bare mound of her abdomen. The baby moved suddenly, forcefully, as if woken from a sound sleep, and Flora looked at her husband and smiled, and saw his face transformed— transfigured.

He bent his head and put his cheek against her belly, and she felt his tears on her skin.

He said, brokenly, 'Flora—oh, Flora *mia*, I love you so much. These last months have been a nightmare. I could not reach you. I thought I never would. That you would never want to be my wife, no matter how I longed for you. That even when our child was born you might not turn to me.'

He took a deep breath. '*Mia cara*, can you ever forgive the wrong I did you and let me be your husband in truth? I swear I will spend the rest of my life trying to make you happy.'

She ran a caressing hand over his dishevelled hair. 'I think I might.' Her voice trembled into a smile. 'If you'll kiss me, and tell me again that you love me.'

He raised his head sharply, his eyes scanning her face. He said her name, then his mouth was on hers, passionately, tenderly, in a kiss that was also a vow.

A long time later, she said, 'Why aren't you in Milan?'

'What a question, *mia bella*,' Marco said lazily. 'Anyone would think you were not pleased to see me.' He'd managed somehow to squeeze himself on to the narrow bed beside her, and was lying with her wrapped in his arms and her head on his chest.

'I am,' she said. 'But I'd still like a straight answer.'

He was silent for a moment. '*Cara*, I have thought about you every day we have been apart, but today it was different. From the moment I awoke this morning I had this strange feeling that you needed me, that I should come to you. And then Alfredo telephoned me, as usual, and told me that Tonio and Ottavia had returned and were staying at the villa. I knew my instinct was right and I should come home at once.'

Ottavia, thought Flora in horror, remembering that briefly glimpsed face at the wheel of the car.

She must have tensed, because he said at once, 'Is something wrong?'

It might have been, she thought. But it wasn't. Because if Ottavia had been tempted to run her down she'd pulled out at the last moment. Perhaps it was enough for her to know that the girl she hated had taken a dive into the mud.

Whatever, she thought, it's because of her that Marco is here with me now. And because of that I can forgive her anything. So I'll keep her secret. Because she has caused enough trouble and I only want to be happy.

Aloud, she said, 'I didn't know Alfredo phoned you each day.'

'I needed to ask about you, *mia cara*. To make sure you were well, and perhaps happy. All the questions I dared not ask you.' He sighed. 'Every time we were together I wanted to fall on my knees in front of you and beg for another chance, but I was afraid I would just make you angry, and that you would use that as an excuse to leave me again.'

She said gently, 'I think I forgave you a long time ago. And, whatever your motivation, it brought us together. I can't forget that.'

'Yet it so nearly did not,' he said slowly. 'When I first came to England I was very angry. Your former *fidanzato* had done great damage to the Baressi family, and to the girl to whom I was reluctantly engaged.'

He shook his head. '*Dio*, Ottavia was hysterical—threatening suicide. And then there was my godmother, telling me with every breath it was my duty to avenge Ottavia's honour, and mine.'

'Were you very fond of her?'

'I was grateful. She could be kind, especially when my parents died. But not fond. She was too cold a woman.'

'So why did you agree to this revenge scheme?'

He said ruefully, 'Because she gave me no peace, and also I felt this Cristoforo deserved to be punished.'

He paused. 'And I felt guilty too, for asking Ottavia to marry me for no better reason than it had always been expected of us. She knew that I did not love her, and I think was hurt by it. This may have driven her to behave as she did. She wanted attention, and sex, and the appearance of love—and she had none of them from me. So she looked for them elsewhere and found Cristoforo, who did not love her either.

'It was Ottavia who insisted that any form of revenge should involve you, because you were the reason Cristoforo had left her. But by the time I reached England I'd had time to think, and I decided that I would pursue your *fidanzato* only. Attack him financially, and ruin him.'

'So why did you change your mind?' Flora asked.

He said slowly, 'Because I was curious. The detective I had engaged had tracked you down, and I went to the restaurant where you were having lunch in order to see the girl who had been preferred to Ottavia.'

He paused. 'And when I saw you, *mia bella*, I wanted you so badly that it scared me, because I had never felt like that for any woman before. And, if I am being honest, I did not want to feel it for you. I told myself that to have you would be the quickest way to cure myself of such a need. So—I reverted to my original plan.'

She sighed. 'And I just—fell into your hand.'

He put his lips remorsefully to the curve of her cheek. 'But I was not cured, *carissima*. And the more I tried to satisfy my appetite for you, the hungrier I got. And it wasn't just your body I wanted, either. I found I was longing to protect you and cherish you for my whole life. I wanted you as my wife, and the mother of my children.'

His voice hardened. 'And I was even more determined to take you away from your *fidanzato* because I knew he would never love you as I did.

'Then, after the plan had worked, it was too late to tell you the truth, because I was scared I would lose you. So I took the coward's way out and said nothing, and lost you anyway.'

'But you came after me,' she reminded him gently. 'That wasn't cowardly.'

He winced. 'But it was the worst day of my life, *cara*. Because I could see how I had hurt you—and that you hated me for it. And I was helpless. There was no excuse I could make for what I had done. Not then—because you would not have listened.'

He cupped her chin in his hand. 'But what I came to tell you, my darling one, and what you have to know and believe, is that I did not take you for revenge alone, but because I could not live without you.'

He bent his head, and his mouth was gentle as it took hers for a long moment.

When her breathing had steadied again, she said, 'If the phone hadn't rung when it did, would you have gone—walked out of my life?'

'I told myself so,' he admitted. 'But in my heart I

knew that I would keep trying to get you back. And then, by a miracle, I was given another chance.'

'But you were so cold,' she said. 'So businesslike with your terms.'

'I was in shock,' Marco told her frankly. 'And I was angry, too, because I knew that if I had not heard that message you would not have told me about our baby. And that hurt.'

'I've thought all this time that you regretted marrying me,' she said. 'You spent so much time away from me in Milan—I thought perhaps you'd found someone else.'

He gave a low laugh. 'Because of that stupid thing I said? I told you, Flora *mia*, I was hurt, and I wanted to hit back. And also to see if I could make you jealous a little, because that would mean that you cared. And I was ready to clutch at any straw.'

She pulled a face. 'I cared as much as you could ever have wanted,' she told him candidly.

'But not as much as I did, I think.' His voice was rueful, self-accusatory. '*Dio*, I was even jealous of your poor Mutt.'

'Marco!' Flora gave a gurgle of laughter. 'You can't be serious.'

'I grudged him every kind word. That was when I decided, for my own sanity, to stay away from the *castello* and stop torturing myself.'

'And I was so lonely,' she said. 'I needed some kind of outlet for all the love I had pent up inside me. You don't still dislike him, do you?'

'On the contrary, I am grateful to him. It was his howling that gave us a clue where to find you, and then he came running out of the darkness and led us back to you.' He paused. 'But I have no plans to allow him to sleep on our bed, *mia cara*, as I am told he does on yours. I am not that magnanimous.'

She gave him a demure look from under her lashes. 'Are you suggesting, *signore*, that you and I should share a bed again?'

'I do not suggest, *signora*. I demand. I need to hold you in my arms at night to convince myself that my other miracle has been granted.' His voice sank to a whisper. 'That you love me, *carissima*, and want to be with me.'

She put up a hand and stroked his face, smoothing away the lines of strain and weariness, her eyes luminous with tenderness.

She said softly, 'For the rest of my life, my dearest love.'

The world's bestselling romance series.

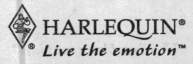

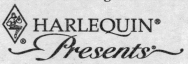

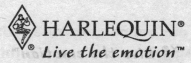

The world's bestselling romance series.

HARLEQUIN®
Presents·

Seduction and Passion Guaranteed!

Back by popular demand...

EXPECTING

*She's sexy,
successful
and
PREGNANT!*

Relax and enjoy our fabulous series about
couples whose passion results in
pregnancies...sometimes unexpected! Of
course, the birth of a baby is always a joyful
event, and we can guarantee that our
characters will become besotted moms and
dads—but what happened in those nine
months before?

Share the surprises, emotions, drama and
suspense as our parents-to-be come to terms
with the prospect of bringing a new life into
the world. All will discover that the business
of making babies brings with it the most
special love of all....

Our next arrival will be

PREGNANCY OF CONVENIENCE
by Sandra Field
On sale June, #2329

**Pick up a Harlequin Presents® novel and you will enter a world
of spine-tingling passion and provocative, tantalizing romance!**

Available wherever Harlequin books are sold.

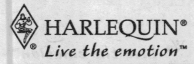

HARLEQUIN®
Live the emotion™

Visit us at www.eHarlequin.com

HPEXPJA

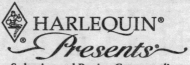

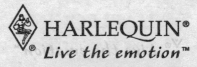

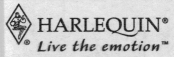